MW00426110

HEY, BROWN GIRL

A Novel

Janay Harden

Hey, Brown Girl

Copyright © 2020 by Janay Harden

All rights reserved

This book or any portion thereof may not be reproduced or used in any manner whatsoever without the express written permission of the author and publisher except for the use of brief quotations in a book review.

Printed in the United States of America

First Printing, 2021

ISBN 978-1-7365412-0-3

Published by: NS Publishing Company

www.theauthorstrategist.com

Thank you for choosing to read "Hey, Brown Girl." I hope you find something within this book you can take with you for years to come.

Please join my email list by scanning the QR code or going to www.naywrites.com for notifications of new releases.

To my favorite brown girl, Zoe: May you do everything with what you're given and be your own best thing.

CHAPTER 1

Raven stood there.

Up against the wall in her bathroom. She held her head. She felt warm, dizzy. *Breathe Raven, breathe,* she willed. *Calm your body.* Raven felt a drop of sweat trickle down her left eyebrow and knew it was coming. Her neck heaved back and forth, and she tasted the saliva collecting in the back of her throat. She tried to force the bile down, but it was too late. It surged through her belly. Raven leaned over the toilet and dry heaved the contents of her stomach into the bowl. She was still coughing and spitting. Her stomach continued contracting while she held the wall to steady herself.

"Great first day of school," she muttered. Eleventh grade began today.

"Are you okay?" Her mom half knocked; half rushed in — her eyes were wide with concern.

"I'm fine, Mom, I'm good," she said, hoping her stomach settled. She brushed her teeth and then rinsed her mouth with Listerine. Raven's mom continued to stare at her.

"Baby girl. What's this about?"

Raven rushed into her room, looking for the clothes she had picked out the night before. She stopped for a second and sat down on her bed and rubbed her head. She was doing too much.

Raven examined her nails carefully, having already looked at them a million times since yesterday. They were bright yellow with one finger on each hand, painted with a leopard design. Raven looked over at her Mom as she was still studying her. Her eyes roamed her body and made Raven anxious. Raven was always anxious these days, hence the vomiting on the first day of school. Her mom moved from the armchair and plopped down on her bed. She wore her hair in wine-red Sister locks, a t-shirt that said, "Nothing For Us Without Us." Her jeans were ripped at the knee. She glanced at her mom and assumed she had an event at the art gallery where she worked. She always wore statement t-shirts when she did. Her mom had golden-brown freckles scattered across her face and neck. She had slanted eyes that sometimes made her look Egyptian. She was slim, which they all found to be funny because she refused to exercise. She claimed she was always "too busy" for exercise with a flutter of her hands. She said her mom used to always say, "Women should only break a sweat doing one thing."

Gross.

But that's her mom: Blair Jamison, a cussing, bangle-wearing, incense-lighting, Mama. She was beautiful. Raven had her mom's freckles but hated her own. They looked great on Blair, not Raven. She found herself many times searching her own face, looking for features that matched. The curves in her nose, her naturally long lashes, and unruly eyebrows.

"What Black girl has freckles?" she would ask.

"One the Sun and Ancestors themselves kissed," Blair always replied.

"Rayyyy!"

Raven heard her voice before she saw her. The front door slammed shut, and Nana came running up the steps barging in.

"Hello to you, too, Nana!" Blair screamed back, passing each other in the hallway.

"Hey baby, besos!" Nana said to Blair. Raven rolled her eyes with anticipation and amusement. Nana had arrived in the building. Raven waited on the bed for Phoenix Harris-her Nana. She half-knocked, half-walked into the room, and Raven chuckled. It was a family trait.

Nana was now in her 50s with skin smooth like honey. She slathers on shea butter like it was the fountain of youth. She cut her hair down super low and dyed it honey blonde. Nana sported some scars on her forearms from fights when she was a kid. Today, Nana wore a tight Adidas track suit from head to toe with matching sneakers, a sparkly fanny pack, and a sun visor.

“Where you heading, Nana?” Raven asked, looking her up and down.

“Me and Johnny Gil got my Yoga class this morning, girl,” Nana said.

That’s right. Raven forgot Nana took on an additional yoga class she taught at the Lacroix YMCA. John is Nana’s White boyfriend, but she called him Johnny Gil because Nana said when John first saw Nana, he rubbed his hands together and said, *“My, my, my,”* or so the story goes. Raven thought this was funny. He seemed so straightlaced, and he only wore button-up shirts with loafers. It always amused Blair when he came around too. She said he reminded her of an accountant.

“I just came to say have a great first day, baby. Me and John are rooting for you. I lit some candles last night, and well, don’t worry about it,” she said, swatting Raven away. “It’s handled.” Raven chuckled to herself. Nana is so crazy.

“Besos,” she said to Raven, blowing kisses and shutting the door behind her. The front door opened, and Nana ran outside where Johnny Gil sat waiting in the car. He waved, and Nana blew more kisses before they pulled off.

“Is dad here?” Raven screamed down to Blair. She began dressing.

“He already left for the morning, but he said check your phone before you go,” Blair screamed back.

Raven grabbed her phone and began scrolling until she found a video from her Dad. Khalil was dressed in his Lake Lacroix police uniform. He is one of the few Black officers in the city, and Raven worried about him often.

The night before, Khalil came home blasting *"Back that Azz Up"* from the radio. A true NOLA classic. He booty bumped her right there, and Blair giggled like a schoolgirl as she swatted him with the dishrag. Sometimes these two could be so cheesy. Raven scrolled through the pictures on her phone, and she landed on a picture of her Aunt Cocina, her Dad's younger sister. Yes, Cocina is her name.

Khalil had told Raven the story many times. He had lived in Arizona as a kid, and Cocina was conceived in a kitchen, so she was named after it. Nana had been in her Mexican food phase back then. He sounds disgusted every time he tells that story, which isn't that often, but Raven found it funny. She enjoyed when Aunt Cocina came over. Cocina had this loud raspy voice, and she resembled Khalil except with lipstick and a cigarette hanging out of her mouth. Aunt Cocina was animated and always said exactly what she was thinking; Raven's mom had quietly disclosed to Raven that Aunt Cocina was in foster care for a few years when Khalil was away in college. Cocina was on and off drugs starting at age sixteen, and things had been a struggle since then. He always asked about Carter, Cocina's son. Carter was eight, and they didn't spend a lot of time with him since he and Cocina always seemed to be on the move. More importantly, he knew how to work every nerve and put the others on layaway for the next visit. He was also glued to the Xbox game and refused to eat with the family or do much of anything.

"She's ruining him," Blair would say. Khalil said nothing about Aunt Cocina.

Raven snapped out of her thoughts and pressed play on her dad's video. He was silly dancing to Beyoncé's *"Brown Skin Girl."* Khalil was standing outside of Dunkin Donuts, singing in the parking lot. Raven grinned. Khalil's voice cracked as he struggled to hit the notes. He feigned a fake cough.

"Baby girl I want you to have a strong first day, and I'll see you at home. Make today count!" He now sipped his water bottle and cleared his throat.

Raven's eyes sparkled. Her dad was unproblematic, and her mom was free-spirited, creative. A self-proclaimed Feminist. Her dad was straightlaced and fun. He loved cars, dancing, and he made them stop for every old junker on the street he thought he could fix up. The three of them together were a team and made each other better. No one got left behind.

Raven examined her face in her bedroom mirror and eyed pictures of her friends. She had many photos, some with dog ears, halos, lips, and various filters the girls used. They were all carefully placed in the corners of Raven's mirror, so she saw them every morning when she dressed. Raven beamed. Her girls: Nia Stewart, Jasmine Ericks, and Trinity Tyrell called themselves the Brown Girls Club. Raven wasn't sure where the name came from, but it felt good to be a part of it. Raven searched for her Brown Girls Club jacket, which she found, hanging over the corner of her bed. She laid it out. Blair bought all the girls matching jackets for Christmas two years ago. Blair was so proud of them and made sure the girls knew they were all celebrated and not overlooked. Raven wrung her hands, remembering she hung her clothes in the bathroom. She pulled them down from behind the bathroom door, scolding herself for forgetting. She had stood in her bedroom closet the night before just a few hours ago, worrying about what clothes to wear. Blair suggested a few items, and soon they had an outfit. Throwing looks together came easily to Blair. Raven wore jean overalls with pink Airmax sneakers and a "Be You" necklace. Her hair was big and curly, with all different sizes and shaped ringlets falling at her shoulders. Her hair always got bigger and bigger as the day went on until it covered her face, cheeks, and forehead. She liked it that way. No, she preferred it that way. Raven had braces that lined her mouth, and she hated to smile and have people notice them. She only had about two more months to go before they could come off, and she was waiting patiently. Raven is short, only standing about five-foot-two, even. Raven looked at herself in the mirror one more time and ran her hands up and down her waist; she didn't have hips. Not like her mom. She didn't have a butt or breasts either, at least not like her friends. When Raven was in the fifth grade, the boys during recess used to scream '*Here comes Bones!*' and fall out laughing. Nia had come from somewhere and pushed one of the boys onto a mound of dirt, which his friends found equally hilarious. It seemed like Nia had come into Raven's life quickly, haphazardly. Although no words were spoken between the girls at that moment, Raven felt like Nia had taken her hand and told her that things would be okay — and they were okay. The day always stuck out in her mind. Her Brown Girls Club was all she needed.

Raven finished dressing and ran downstairs while Blair sat out a bowl of oatmeal for breakfast.

"You look great, pretty girl. How do you feel?"

"I'm okay." Raven's voice cracked. Blair must've sensed her apprehension.

"I have something for you," she said, handing Raven a small box. She opened the box, and there sat a pair of earrings in Raven's favorite shade of amber yellow. The earrings had a picture of a Sunflower, and under the Sunflower in small words, it said: *Even tucked away, I still bloom.*

"You make your reality, pretty girl. Now you go bloom. Keep that in mind when you feel anxious."

"I love it, Mom!" Raven beamed. And she did. Her mom was always reading her mind with things like this. Raven finished her oatmeal, and she began walking to the bus stop.

"Wait!" Blair yelled from the house and hustled towards Raven. "I'll walk with you," Blair said. Raven didn't mind. Her mom was good company. Raven looked around and patiently waited for Nia to arrive.

They all lived on The Hill. Nia lived at the end of the block with her mom, Ms. Tina, and younger brother Bryce. They lived in Lake Lacroix, Louisiana, a bayou town nestled right next door to NOLA. People were always trying to move away, but for Raven, it was perfect. The weather was always balmy, bouncing between seventy and eighty degrees, and large oak trees lined the streets to our shotgun style homes. The city is "*Black Black*", as Blair liked to call it, and she even attended the historically black college of Xavier University, where Blair was loud and proud of all things Black. Their family bought everything from Black-owned businesses, and they did their best to support their people. It was everything to Raven.

Raven spotted Nia running out of the house with Ms. Tina and Bryce. Ms. Tina was always dressed up, and she made sure Nia always was too.

“Girl, what are you over there thinking about?!” Nia said, bouncing over to Raven’s side with her mom.

“Nothing hush. . . Look at you. Okay, Nia!” The fashionista in Nia stayed with a bright color palette. Raven glanced her over. Raven preferred her own hair out and wild — she hated for her scalp to be smothered under braids. Nia’s hair was braided all the way down to her back with braids blue and some yellow. The color of their school mascots. Nia’s edges were perfectly laid, and she was wearing a blue and white tie-dyed short set. Her skin was a pretty shade of Mocha, like Normani, and she could sing better than anyone in our school. She was Raven’s best friend.

“You better be you!” Blair exclaimed. Raven eyed her mom, eying Nia. She felt a twinge of jealousy as her mom could never quite find the source of Raven’s anxiety. It just seemed to always be there, rearing its ugly head at the most inopportune times. Whereas Nia was proud to stand out, Raven tried to stand out of the way.

Nia beamed with pride back at Blair. Nothing pleased her more than receiving compliments about her clothes and singing. Raven and Nia were on the Lake Lacroix dance team together. Although Nia was a better singer, Raven was the better dancer. Raven was also the Lake Lacroix dance team captain.

Khalil would say, “Mom has art, and I have cars.” He told Raven she had to find her *thing,* but she didn’t even know what her *thing* was. Sometimes she believed that it was dancing.

If I could just get over my nerves, she thought, as she bit the inside of her cheek. She got so shy when she knew people were watching and critiquing. It wasn’t the watching part that bothered her. No, that wasn’t it. Raven knew that she could dance — that wasn’t up for debate. But she didn’t like when people critiqued her moves, compared and contrasted the girls next to each other. People were always searching for a top dog out of the group. The girls made sure they mostly shined together, but people had a way of ruining beautiful things, and sometimes teenagers could be the worst of them all. Hence, Raven’s apprehension about people’s assessment of their group.

The bus stop filled up with anxious students and their parents as the bus crept its way down the street.

“Hurry girls stand together for a picture,” Ms. Tina said. Raven and Nia huddled together and said, “cheeeese.”

“This one is for Facebook!” Ms. Tina declared. Ms. Tina and Nia both loved social media. Ms. Tina says it’s the perfect way to fight injustices because, “Everyone has a social media account, and instead of fussing, they should make it their message.”

Nia liked social media because she could make singing videos. Raven could take it or leave it.

The bus pulled up at that moment, and Ms. Twizz opened the door with a bright smile, “Mais cher, I’ve missed you!” she shouted.

Ms. Twizz had been with them since the 6th grade. Every year Ms. Twizz gave out Twizzlers and other candy on the bus. One student began calling her Ms. Twizzler, and that was when the name was born. Initially, they believed the name would upset Ms. Twizz, and she for sure would get them in trouble for bullying. But Ms. Twizz proclaimed, “Nope, honey, Imma make it easy for you an’em. Call me Ms. Twizz.” From that moment on, they did. Ms. Twizz was an older Black woman, and she kept her long nails painted with different colors every week, and she loved reggae music on the bus. Ms. Twizz is from Bacakatown, a section of NOLA, but she told us her “spirit animal is from Jamaica.”

Blair and Raven saw her in the Piggly Wiggly a few weeks ago. She said to Blair, “Honey, the teachers an’em ain’t got nothing on me. My job is the most important one of all, and that’s keeping these kids safe.” This seemed to please Blair, but Raven was too busy looking into Ms. Twizz’s basket to see if she was buying candy. Sure enough, Ms. Twizz was handing out Twizzlers today. The girls got onto the bus and happily accepted their candies. They were the last stop on the bus, so Ms. Twizz always gave them extra.

"How's ya mama, an'em?" Ms. Twizz asked.

"Everyone is a'ight," Raven replied, speaking for Nia too.

Raven and Nia sat in separate seats across from each other. Raven waved to her mom as the door closed, and she began eating her Twizzler. Nia was still taking pictures.

"Y'all sit back and relax, don't worry, be happy Mon!" Ms. Twizz called out as she closed the door and pulled off slowly.

CHAPTER 2

The girls arrived at Lake Lacroix High School and shuffled inside with Nia snapping selfies. Raven looked around for the other ladies, and waiting in the corridor was Jasmine Ericks.

Jasmine stood taller than the rest of the group, commanding silent attention. She was light brown-skinned with high cheekbones, and her skin had a natural glow like she had been rolling around on a beach some place. She was a fashionista like Nia, but she preferred name brands. Jasmine played basketball but was the girliest player on the team, always keeping her hair and nails done. Today she wore a sleek, long ponytail touching her mid-back. Her edges were sculpted to her temples. The ponytail swung and stayed in place as Jasmine moved about. Raven knew Jasmine carefully crafted that baby to her head, and she meant business. Raven glanced down at her ratty old Jumper and touched her hair. Now, she didn't feel so dressed to impress. Nia squeezed Raven's hand and whispered, "I love your earrings."

"Thank you," Raven smiled. That's why Nia was her bestie.

Jasmine went to her cousin's house for the summer in Florida, and Raven hadn't seen her in person since tenth grade ended. Jasmine seemed even taller and wore the brightest smile.

"Hey, Brown Girls!" she squealed to Raven and Nia. "I have to tell you something." Her eyes looked worried. Before Raven could ask questions, their other friend Trinity Tyrell walked up.

"Brown Girls!" Trinity screamed.

"Ayyeeee!" The group yelled back. Trinity was here, and they were complete!

Raven studied Trinity. She was wearing a Nike tracksuit, and her hair was pulled tight in a bun — her edges laid to perfection. Out of all the girls, she envied her hair. Trinity never had to do much but spray it with water and brush it down. The girls urged her to wear it out occasionally, but Trinity loved her bun. She was a rich shade of brown and had the smoothest, clearest skin with perfectly arched eyebrows.

"Did you guys check out your schedules? I didn't see any classes together," Trinity said.

"That's what I was going to say!" Jasmine flung her hands. They conferred in the hallway, examining their schedules with laser focus. Raven's heart skipped a beat; they were both right.

"How can this be?" Jasmine's voice was laced with frustration.

Raven had the same questions and wondered if her Dad forgot to drop off her course selection sheet at the beginning of the summer.

"Well, my mom's boyfriend said he heard in the barbershop they had to revise all the classes this year," Trinity said.

The girls groaned and frantically looked again, hunting for any classes they may have together. They found only a few. Raven's stomach hurt again, and beads of sweat threatened to appear at her hairline.

"Guys, we'll be fine. We got this. Okay?" Nia urged. Nia was the yin to Raven's worrying yang; she was always optimistic.

"Okay," the other girls groaned.

The bell sounded, and the girls rushed off in different directions for homeroom. Raven strolled down the hallway, hoping to settle herself before she became even more anxious. Blair told Raven she had to calm her body and guided her through a 5-4-3-2-1 coping technique for anxiety. Raven looked around for five things she could see: *The walls, the oak trees outside, other students, her schedule in her hand, and Mrs. Young, Raven's homeroom teacher.* Raven glanced around for four things she could touch: *Her clothes, her hair, the lockers, and her book bag.* Three things she could hear: *the bell ringing, students laughing, and someone running down the steps behind her.* Two things she could smell: *her vanilla perfume (Blair says all Black girls should smell of vanilla and honey). And popcorn. Raven smelled popcorn.* One thing she could taste. . . *the gum in her mouth.*

She took a deep breath, determined not to let this ruin her day.

Walking into homeroom and slightly late, Raven saw her arch-nemesis: Taylor French. Well, maybe arch nemesis was intense, but honey, they just did not get along. She was on the dance team with Raven and Nia, and Taylor was always trying to outdo them. Everything Raven had; Taylor sought to undermine! Taylor was about Raven's height and complexion with smooth honey-brown skin and long black hair. It always looked so perfect and put together. Raven sat down across the class from Taylor so she couldn't see Raven roll her eyes. Raven looked over and noticed a new face in the classroom. A new boy and .... my God. . . he was gorgeous. Raven looked at him. She had never seen such rich skin, he looked like milk chocolate. His eyes pierced her soul, and he had the most beautiful lashes she had ever seen on a boy. They looked even better than Nia's mom's lashes, and she got hers done every week!

Khalil loves listening to Tupac, and he's always rapping, "the darker the berry, the sweeter the juice." Khalil always rapped that part extra hard when it came on. Raven understood what he meant in that moment. The berry was indeed dark and beautiful.

"Raven Jamison? Raven Jamison?" Raven heard her name being called, and she jerked out of her trance to Mrs. Young staring at her.

"Are we here or not today, Ms. Raven?"

"I'm here," Raven sheepishly shrank in her seat.

"You are late." Mrs. Young asserted.

Raven watched Taylor in the front of the class snicker with her minions she calls friends, Jessica Bryant, and Brianna Cummings.

"Thank you for being here with us, Ms. Jamison," Mrs. Young says as she side-eyed Raven.

"Amir Langston?" she called from her clipboard.

The handsome creature sitting next to her she had been staring at said

"Here."

Amir Langston. That was his name. It sounded beautiful too. Raven's stomach seemed like it was at the top of a roller coaster. Her mouth was parched. Amir looked over at her and smiled. They sat in the back of the class, and Raven could see Taylor in the front turned around and rolling her eyes in Raven's direction.

The bell rang, and soon, they were off to their classes for the day. Raven was still bummed that she didn't have any classes with her friends, but when she walked into chemistry class with

Mr. Fritzel, she noticed Amir there too. Mr. Fritzel loved to show his classes pictures of all his cats he lived with at home. He must have had dozens of them. He came to school with cat hair all over himself, and he reminded Raven of The Nutty Professor. Mr. Fritzel informed the class they would end the semester by presenting a science project. Great. Now she had a few months to dread the science project with all those people watching. Again, she wished she had at least this class with her girls. Raven knew that together they could kill that project. Students could not have their phones out during the day, so Raven couldn't even text them to check-in.

There had been a "Lids and Lips" challenge, which started on Tik Tok last year. Students recorded themselves licking toilet seats to see who could last the longest. Since then, they permitted no cell phones at school during the day. Raven found the whole thing stupid and never did the challenge. Nia did it, and she said gained lots of new followers. Raven didn't have many followers. If she had to lick a toilet to gain followers, well, she thought it said a lot about her *and* the people following her.

CHAPTER 3

Rumbling noises escaped Raven's stomach throughout the morning. They were so loud she was sure the rest of her classes heard it too. The bell rang, and students shuffled into the hallway heading to the lunchroom, where Raven ran into her girls! Nia walked from the left, with Jasmine and Trinity coming up from the right; the ladies met in the middle. Raven loved when all her girls came together. Even though they're not considered popular like Taylor and her crew, her friends were all she needed. They trekked to the lunchroom, all different shades of brown between them.

Walking in, Raven noticed they were only allowed to sit three to a table. The usual was four to a table, and four was what they needed.

"Guys, I'll sit at a table right next to you. It's no big deal." Trinity offered. Raven studied Trinity. "Are you sure?"

"No, guys, seriously, it's fine. You know I like my space, anyway." Trinity was right. Whenever they had sleepovers, Trinity preferred to sleep on the floor by herself. If they were going out somewhere and planned to get dressed together, she usually came already dressed and just waited for the rest of them to finish. She marched to her own beat and did her own thing.

"Okay," Nia said hesitantly.

Half of the Brown Girls Club sat down at their table while Trinity sat alone next to them. While in line, Raven overheard their Vice Principal, Mrs. Beckett, tell another student they were hoping with the new seating arrangements, lunchroom fights would decrease. Raven had to admit, there were a lot of food fights. She was in the middle of deciding if she would eat the cold hamburger for lunch or wait until she got home when she heard the angels sing above.

"Is this seat taken?"

Raven looked over, and sure enough, there he stood. Amir asked Trinity if he could sit at her table. Trinity sat unfazed by his beauty while Raven was dumbstruck.

"Sure." Trinity didn't even look up at him, and she motioned with her hand for him to sit.

His eyes seem to shine a little brighter this time. Raven studied his features. He had high cheekbones with soft dreadlocks surrounding his face. Raven hadn't noticed those dreads before; she was too busy staring at his eyes. He was wearing a crisp Adidas t-shirt with khaki shorts and Adidas sneakers. Around his neck hung a small gold pendant. Raven looked closely and saw it was a picture of Africa. Raven only saw him in homeroom, but now Raven fully *saw* him. He was beautiful. Raven realized she was holding her breath when Nia kicked her under the table. *"Get yourself together,"* she mouthed.

Raven observed the cafeteria. This was the only time students were permitted to use their phones, and everyone sat eating and scrolling. She checked her own phone and scrolled for a second but found nothing that interested her. She only had a Tik Tok and IG account anyway, while her friends had all the things: Snapchat, IG, FB, Tik Tok, and a bunch of others that she couldn't keep up with. Raven's eyes settled on Taylor, Jessica, and Brianna sitting in the lunchroom corner. Taylor was sitting on the edge of the table telling a story. Taylor leaned over to Jessica, and they turned their heads, quickly glancing in Amir's direction.

Raven's nerves set in again. She hoped Taylor wasn't setting her sights on Amir. He wasn't even her type! Taylor's latest boyfriend was Justin, the captain of the Lake Lacroix football team. Justin was dense, and Raven was pretty sure a potted plant was smarter. Justin and Raven had one class together last year when they partnered for the spelling bee. His word was "xylophone," and don't you know, Genius Justin stuttered and stammered over his word before so eloquently misspelling it. *"Z, y.. . ."* Justin started. Raven was mortified.

Vocabulary was her specialty, and he ruined their chances at winning the competition. Justin had the nerve to go back and tell everyone it was Raven's fault they lost because she didn't practice the word with him. Raven made a mental note to see if she and Justin had any classes together, she didn't want any mishaps again.

"Where are you from? You just moved here, right?" Raven heard from the other table.

"Yeah," Amir turned to Trinity. "My mom says this is a better school district to help me get into a private school for college. I play basketball, and I'm trying to get a scholarship."

He plays basketball. Raven wondered how that would work. Their boys' basketball team had been notoriously bad for years. Last year the team was so awful they forfeited at least two games. They were getting beat like they stole something, but maybe he would change that soon.

"Hi there."

Taylor's voice made Raven's stomach sink.

"I just wanted to come and introduce myself. My name is Taylor, these are my friends Jessica and Brianna. If you need help with anything, just let me know." Taylor stood in the front with her minions behind her on each side. "I'm friends with just about everyone here," she side-eyed Raven's table.

Raven watched Nia — who was looking at Jasmine. Jasmine and Raven shared the same intense dislike for Taylor, so Raven knew Nia was trying to calm her down. Raven had her own reasons for disliking Taylor, but Jasmine's mom used to be a maid in Taylor's house. Taylor didn't know Jasmine was the maid's daughter, and Jasmine didn't know it was Taylor's house she was going to help her mom for the day. Once Taylor saw Jasmine at the house, it seemed like she set her sights on her for a while and told people that she was *the help.* She and Taylor have come to blows many times over that one.

"Thank you, it's nice to meet you all," Amir replied. He was so polite. Taylor would ruin him.

The bell rang, and Raven rushed off to Math class. Amir walked in not long after Raven, and he quietly sat down beside her.

"Okay, guys, we're going to pair up and do a 'getting-to-know-you' exercise. Pair up with the person next to you and complete this worksheet." Mr. Smith handed out papers.

"Let's see how we are all similar and how we're different," Mr. Smith called out. Raven rolled her eyes. This was busy work, and Mr. Smith knew it. What did it even have to do with Math? And Amir was the person sitting right next to her. *Here we go,* she thought.

"Hi, I'm Amir .... Raven, right?"

"Yes." Raven mustered, swallowing the ever-present lump in her throat. "You're new here, right?" Raven tried to sound cool.

"Yeah, my mom, and my sister moved from Easton. This school is a lot different."

"Yea, I bet. How so?"

"For starters, I didn't know hanging at the car wash was an event." Amir chuckled.

Raven squealed and covered her mouth. "You're so wrong for that!" Amir nailed it. The car wash was a hangout spot in town, and sometimes the girls and Raven rode their bikes the three-mile trek to sit and spy cars moving about. Some were washing their cars, but most were there to flex in front of everyone. They sold anything you could think of mixtapes, incense, weed, jewelry, fake Nike slides, candles. Scores of food trucks lined the parking lot every weekend. Raven's dad even visited; he rode through with his souped-up old Cutlass grinning from ear to ear.

"Who else do you live with?"

"Just my mom and sister. My dad is in prison."

"I'm-I'm so sorry," Raven stuttered. She could kick herself for even asking.

"Na, you're good. He's been there a long time, it's cool."

Raven was mortified, for the second time that day.

"So, basketball, huh?" Raven now chose her words carefully and didn't know what to say. Why did he make her so nervous?

"Yea, that's my thing, I guess," he shrugged. As Raven contemplated what to say next, Amir said, "Nice earrings. My mom is into sunflowers, she would love those."

"Thanks, my mom got them for me," Raven blurted.

Maybe Nia was right, and Raven was hard on herself for no reason. *"Be you, let the world adjust,"* she always said. Nia's words were so similar to Blair's. It seemed like everyone always knew what to say and how to say it regarding Raven's life. She knew that they were right, in some way. But some things just took time, and she was one of those people who always had to learn the hard way before it really stuck. Amir and Raven finished the rest of the worksheet, and she learned a lot about Amir. His mom was a social worker down at the Lakes Hospital, and he has one younger sister Aamani.

"Okay, class, time is up," Mr. Smith announced.

One by one, they went around the room sharing what they learned about their partner during the exercise. When it was their turn, Amir said "This is Raven. She is an only child, and she likes sunflowers, dancing, and ice cream."

Raven stood next.

"This is Amir, he transferred from Easton High School. He plays basketball, he loves math and fried chicken." The class laughed.

Someone in the back screamed, “drums or flats!?” The class erupted in banter, debating which was better. Once someone explained to Mr. Smith what drums and flats were, he nosedived into a ten-minute speech about how scientifically the drums have more meat and therefore — are better, he concluded.

We all roared with laughter.

“Mr. Smith, how could you . . drums really!?” Someone called out.

“I don’t know Mr. Smith, the way the ranch dressing coats the flat wings, it’s a game changer for me,” another classmate admitted.

“Yea, drums could never!” A girl screamed in the back. Raven looked around. This was great and unexpected. She usually would be too nervous to engage in class wide discussions like this, but she felt good today and wished Nia was here to see.

CHAPTER 4

“Hurry up, girl, it’s hot out here!” Nia yelped as Raven made it closer to the bus after the last bell rang. She hurried her pace as they got on the bus and greeted Ms. Twizz.

“My Brownies, how was your first day?” Ms. Twizz’s eyes were wide and ready. They looked like they had been waiting all day to ask their questions and see what they saw.

“Mine was okay. Raven and I don’t have any classes together. And you remember Josue? From last year? He’s in like three of my classes, and he’s still trying to be a rapper!” Nia huffed.

Raven giggled to herself.

“Taylor is in my homeroom, and did you see that new boy? Amir? Well, he’s in my homeroom, math, and chemistry class.”

“Oh, is he now?” Nia smirked at Raven. Raven turned away, avoiding Nia’s eyes.

“Amir, huh?” Ms. Twizz turned down her music.

She passed back some Starburst candies for us. In four years, Raven never mentioned a boy, and that alone led Ms. Twizz to believe Raven didn’t care any which way. She seemed to view them as dispensable; her words were usually laced with disdain and a list of things they had done to her. Raven glanced around on the bus.

The other students lay hunched over, some sleeping.

"So, homeroom, math, and what other class did you say?" Ms. Twizz repeated.

"Chemistry."

"And lunch," Nia added.

"Oh yes, lunch." Raven almost forgot about that one.

"That's not bad. Could be worse. Could have every single class together all day long. That would be too much!" Ms. Twizz snapped her fingers.

Hmmm. Raven hadn't thought about that. She's right, it could be worse. She could've had classes with Amir all day. She for sure would've been a Nervous Nelly if that happened. Raven relaxed some on the ride home. Someone in the back of the bus started playing music, and she heard Wild Wayne's voice from Q93. She heard the beats get louder and louder, and she nodded her head. She looked over at Nia and who was still scrolling through her phone. Raven could make out the Instagram reflection shining her eyes.

"Jasmine says meet at City Park with your bike at 4. Did she text you?"

Raven checked her phone, and sure enough, Jasmine had texted her.

"Do you think Trinity is coming too?" Raven asked. She didn't feel like smelling Trinity's nine-year-old brother Austin.

Trinity had to watch him because her mom was often working down at The Bayou Restaurant in town. Austin could be considered the most annoying, smelliest kid ever. Wrestling seemed to be his claim to fame. Raven didn't understand it and didn't want to. He even wore those little wrestling outfits that the pros had. No way, Jose.

Seconds later, Raven's phone buzzed, and a text from Trinity said that she had to bring her brother because her mom was working. Raven groaned to herself, and the girls looked at each other. Thinking the same thing, they cracked up. Pulling the door shut from her second to last stop, Nia asked Ms. Twizz to turn up her music. Ms. Twizz obliged.

"Let the smooth Caribbean sounds take you away," Ms. Twizz snapped her fingers. Raven saw Ms. Twizz gyrate her hips in the seat. Ms. Twizz had rhythm. The girls smiled —they loved this time alone with Ms. Twizz.

"How's your Rick doing, Ms. Twizz?" Rick was Ms. Twizz's son. He was twenty when he went to prison for selling weed and had quite a few more years to go. The case angered Ms. Tina and Blair. They spent many afternoons on the phone discussing it and all things Black in America.

"He's doing okay, my Brownies, he's doing okay. One day at a time, and I know the Lord gon' make a way, so I'm not worried because I know I'll see my boy an'em again." Ms. Twizz's voice trailed off and got lower.

"We'll see. They gon' see," she nodded her head.

"Well, tell him my mom is always praying for him," Nia put her phone down. Raven didn't know what to say. She shook her head in agreement too. Rounding the corner to Sycamore Street, Ms. Twizz pulled open her door and let the girls exit.

"See ya tomorrow, my Brownies!" Ms. Twizz smiled. The girls waved goodbye, and she pulled off, turning up her music.

"So how long is it gonna take you to get ready, girl?" Raven turned to Nia. Nia was meticulous about every piece of clothing — even for bike riding.

"I'll meet you in thirty minutes on The Hill. Byyee, girl!" Nia called out as she walked away, a pink Starburst rolling around in her mouth as she unwrapped another. She headed over the slope to her house while Raven walked down the hill to her end of Sycamore Street. The girls lived just a quarter mile from each other. The road had a steep incline in the center between their houses, and they spent afternoons racing their bikes up and down the hill. The neighborhood considered it the meeting spot for everything. It was The Hill.

The Jamison's lived in a yellow two-story shotgun style home and had been there for just over a decade. Large steps stood in the center of the home, leading up to the most beautiful ornate set of double glass doors on the block. A brown lantern storm light hung above. Under their feet, Blair had a custom doormat that said, *"Check 'yo energy."* Again, Blair was an artist — or not an artist — depending on the day and how she felt. Regardless, Blair was an artist, and to her, a good door on a house was like seeing the soul of a home.

Khalil shared with Blair some of his fondest memories of childhood took place when they lived in a shotgun-style house way up on a hill. Khalil never talked about fond childhood memories. More than that, Khalil never talked about any childhood memories, let alone fond ones. When Blair learned this tidbit of information, she made it her business to make sure Khalil and their family lived in a home where he felt safe and comfortable. Where they all felt that way. Greys, with splashes of light blue, painted the Jamison walls. Pictures of them hung everywhere. Blair, Khalil, and Raven at Disney World, ice skating, playing soccer, sleeping, Halloween, school events. Blair filled their dining room with candles, plants, and some kind of snack waiting on the table. The family ate dinner together every night.

No one was home yet, and Raven let herself in with her key. Blair was at the gallery and Khalil at the station. Raven ran up the stairs two at a time towards her room. She changed into a short sleeve tracksuit with her Brown Girls Club jacket. She fixed her hair in the mirror and changed into her sneakers. Pulling the garage door open, she found her bike and pulled it down from the wall. Raven checked her phone. She had about an hour and a half before her mom got home. Perfect, just enough time. Her phone buzzed, and she read the text. Nia was on her way.

Raven ran out the house, and a few minutes later, Nia pulled up with her Brown Girls Club jacket on too. Nia smiled and pedaled in front of Raven. Nia had her music turned up on her phone, and Raven made out Drake's voice. Raven liked to ride in the back. It gave her a chance to look around their neighborhood and really take it all in. She smelled the air and inhaled deep. It was so beautiful to her. The homes on Sycamore Street were all shotgun style with modern flair. While some had the bonus of a garage, others had a large and inviting Creole porch. It was a quiet neighborhood and just thirty minutes away sat their neighbor, New Orleans.

When Khalil and Blair went house hunting, Blair said they were out all day with a realtor. Something was always wrong with each of the homes, and sometimes, Blair didn't even have a reason, she just knew it wasn't *The One*. Khalil went along with Blair's antics, only intervening when he thought something was too expensive. Blair told Raven when they finally turned down Sycamore Street, she could smell chocolate cake. Blair didn't know where the smell came from, or even if she was imagining things. But she knew the smell comforted her, and something in her spirit said *slow down at this one. . .* and so they did.

Raven overheard her parents talking one night about moving to NOLA, but Raven hoped they didn't. NOLA was great, but she loved their town. The city was rich with history. Raven and her girls enjoyed watching the boats come in at the docks, the fisherman looking for crabs and crawfish. There was always some festival, and one of her favorites was the Voodoo Music Experience. It was held during Halloween weekend, and they had the best food. Raven and her parents got dressed up in costumes and went as a family. People wanted to move away from Lake Lacroix, but not her.

Even Blair was proud to tell people their town is almost seventy-five percent Black. "We're the real Chocolate City!" she would say to her friends on the phone.

Raven loved riding her bike past the large oak trees in town. Some of them were so big they created a canopy and lined the streets over her head; they swayed gracefully with the wind. Blair says their ancestors planted those mighty trees generations ago, and their love for Lake Lacroix and this land kept them growing. Coupled with the crickets, lightning bugs, and the sounds of the water coming from Lake Pontchartrain, it created a beautiful mosaic of so many things that Raven loved. It was her home.

The weather was seventy-eight degrees, according to her phone. Nia and Raven raced down the street, weaving in and out of the road. Raven popped wheelies on her bike, and Nia tried to pop wheelies herself, but she wasn't having much luck with her struggling to take selfies at the same time. Raven heard her phone shake in the basket on her bike. She picked it up and tried to read the alert and steer at the same time. She almost swerved into their neighbor a few houses down, Mr. Gerald. He was smack dab in her line of fire, and Raven almost took him out. Mr. Gerald screamed and jumped back with his cane. He caught the corner of the mailbox and yelled, "Watch out, girl!" as she raced by. He steadied himself, and his tiny dog barked at her from the porch.

"Charge it to the game," Raven yelled over her shoulder at Mr. Gerald, and the girls dissolved into a fit of giggles. When Raven balanced herself enough to check her phone, she noticed it was an alert from Instagram. It said, "*@BallerAmir* requests to follow you." Raven's heart skipped a beat. Amir requested to follow her on Instagram. Raven held her phone to her mouth and exhaled. Just then, Jasmine and Trinity rode up on their bikes, both wearing their Brown Girls Club jackets. Trinity's brother Austin was in tow. He was weaving in and out of traffic, daring cars to hit him. Raven pushed the alert from IG out of her mind. She would discuss this with the girls later and wanted to keep the news to herself, just a while longer. The girls arrived at Lake Lacroix, and it was a beautiful day. The fishermen were out towing in crawfish, shrimp, and blue crabs. There was a flurry of activity at the docks, and seas of Black people were rushing in different directions. Lake Lacroix was big business. Jasmine took her phone out and put-on music. Raven heard H.E.R. singing from Jasmine's phone.

"Ayyeee," Trinity stood up and danced.

The girls tossed their bikes and walked past the gravel. The grassy area was a short walk down to an oak tree by the water. The girls didn't go past the rocks, the boats coming in made for rough tide. Nia swayed to the music and bobbed her head. She took out her phone and began recording. Raven was next to feel the music. It wasn't the same for her, she had to really feel the music before she let loose. Her shoulders and legs moved in unison, and she gyrated her waist and grooved. Raven let the music build up in her, and once it did — she knew nothing would slow her down. She stepped out on her own, in front of the group. Trinity and Jasmine moved out of the way, and Nia made sure she kept recording. The Brown Girls Club met Raven with nothing but love.

"Go Raven, go, Raven," they chanted as she showcased her dance skills. A few of the ladies on the docks saw the girls dancing and nodded their heads in approval with smiles.

"Ya'll don't hurt 'em now," one of them said.

The girls giggled and formed a circle around Raven while she tied her hair up. Trinity, Jasmine, and Nia knew what this meant: Raven was about to put on a show, and they needed to move out the way. Raven may have preferred to play the background to her girls — except with dancing. She could always be the superstar but had to get over her nerves and feel it. When Raven heard the music, it was like something or someone came over her, and she just had to move her body. She found herself inside of the circle, and three of the ladies from the docks crept over.

They were fanning themselves but curious to see the young girls move. Within no time, the ladies were dancing with them. Someone gave them cool hand towels, and they were being used to sprinkle water on their faces while they tried keeping up with Raven. When music came on, it transported Raven to another place. Another place where she could be anyone or do anything she liked. An older man sat down beside the circle and played a Djembe drum while the girls danced. The music and the beat of the drum hit Raven square in her chest.

Tipitty, tap, tap, boom! Raven could feel each beat of the drum in her heart, radiating throughout her body. People were cheering and danced around the girls, and smaller dance circles formed next to them. Raven's dancing had turned back the clock, and everyone stopped what they were doing and moved together in unison. Raven embraced it and let the music take control. Her Mom's voice echoed in her head.

"Baby girl, when you dance, you can transport people to another world."

Raven didn't know about all that, but she was definitely feeling this. In the distance, she heard waves crashing as they made their own beat, sometimes matching the sounds of the Djembe drum. She twisted her waist, lifted her arms to the sky, and swung back and forth, listening to all the sounds together. The warm August wind blew lightly, and the air engulfed Raven, cooling her body. She danced against blowing wind, the crashing waves, as the beat of the drums bellowed deeper and deeper in her spirit. Together they created a beautiful song, narrating Raven's graceful movements. She continued to dance as Nia recorded everyone. Older women, younger women, teenagers all swayed, and the men watched. The group seemed to get bigger at the beat of each drum. Raven giggled while showing someone how to do some of her moves. They imitated her, and the woman said she was going to pass out trying to keep up with all of Raven's hopping and shaking.

Jasmine's phone rang, interrupting the festivities and putting an end to the music. "Hello?" She answered, out of breath.

The older ladies sat down to catch their breath, and the crowd thinned out. "Whew chile, thank God that song ended, my knee was about to give out!" Raven heard someone say. The oldest woman in the group hobbled to Raven and stood in front of her. "Baby, you have a gift.... use it without shame." She turned and limped away.

Raven pondered her words as Jasmine walked up with her cell phone. "I have to go, girls." Jasmine's Dad was taking her shopping.

They gathered their things and headed back home. Raven noticed Austin looking at her strange. *What a weirdo,* Raven thought. At least he didn't get too close, so Raven didn't have to smell him this time.

CHAPTER 5

Throwing her bike to the ground, Raven walked into her house and found Blair in the kitchen cooking. She had her music blasting, and Raven could hear Lauryn Hill and Nas singing about if they ruled the world. She smelled her Mom's delightful cooking from the front door, and her stomach growled. She could tell her Mom was in a good mood.

"Where you coming from, baby girl?"

"I texted you and dropped my location."

Blair grabbed her phone and scrolled. She was new to the iPhone world and was still learning to navigate the features.

"How do I find that?" Blair pressed the screen.

Taking her mom's phone, Raven went to her location settings and showed her to track Raven's location. For the third time.

"I missed that, sorry. How was the lake today?" Blair asked.

With a yawn, Raven told her Mom about their dancing and how bookoo people formed a circle around them. Blair listened intently to Raven — she always listened intently. Raven loved that about their relationship, she would drop everything to listen to Raven.

"Ray, I told you, baby girl, you have a gift. People are only telling you what they see, but you have to see it."

"Whatcha cooking, Mom?" Raven changed the subject. She wasn't ready to talk about dancing professionally or in front of large groups of people. Even though she was still on a high from the lake, it also made her feel nervous. She didn't know if people could believe in her that way.

Blair swatted at Raven with a spoon.

"First of all, curry chicken and rice-second, don't be shushing me."

Raven grabbed a cookie from behind her mom's back while Blair yelled-"and stay out them cookies, girl!"

Raven updated Blair about her day, especially about lunch and their different schedules.

"Well, maybe it's for the best. Smaller classes and fewer people in lunch doesn't sound so bad." Blair contended. Raven also informed her about the cold hamburger she refused to eat, and she wondered if she should tell her mom about Amir. Technically, there was nothing to tell, but her heart jumped at the thought. It jumped like the Djembe drum she had just finishing dancing to so effortlessly. What was that feeling? It wasn't one Raven had encountered before.

The girls had been boy-crazed, and Raven met a few boys she spent long summer nights conversing with on the front stoop or exchanging texts with. But mostly, she kept to her friends or herself, where she was comfortable.

This was not a comfortable feeling, and she wasn't even sure what the feeling was. Raven decided not to tell her mom just yet. How could she talk about something out loud when she hadn't even figured out the words in her head? Raven heard the front door close; her dad was home. Mr. Jamison strolled into the kitchen and kissed Blair's forehead and slapped her butt.

"Hey Lover," her mom cooed as she stirred the food on the stove. Raven giggled while Khalil stuck his chest out a little prouder.

"Whatcha cookin' good lookin'?"

"Chicken and rice. Go get changed, it's almost done."

Raven was glad her Dad was home. He made everything better, and they were their best when the three of them were together.

"And how was our first day of school, Ms. Jamison?" Khalil winked at Raven.

"It was fine, slayed a couple of dragons and still made it home in time for dinner. A light day." Her parents burst out laughing, and soon, so did Raven. For someone with bad nerves, Raven's parents didn't know just how accurate the description of her day was.

Raven set the table in the dining room; it was always her job. Her mom used to say when she was younger, she ate dinner with her mom and dad, and they shared their day.

She said, "The world is mean, it's nice to come home to a smile and tell someone about your time away." Khalil was a little indifferent. He would rather be watching a Saints game in front of the TV. But he loved Blair, so he went along with most things. Raven vowed when she got older, she would have dinner together every night, too, like her mom did. Blair lit candles around the dining room and turned off the music. Khalil ran down the stairs, and he was wearing a Lake Lacroix PD t-shirt and ball shorts.

"So, Ms. Jamison, let's huddle up," Khalil teased. He took Raven's fork and began scooping food onto his plate.

"Dad!" Raven yelled, going to get another fork.

Every night for dinner, the family had what they call, Huddle. The trio asked each other to share a high from their day and a low. Blair used to work in a hospital, and she said they held a daily meeting called Huddle to make sure nothing was being overlooked and everyone was communicating. Blair began making her family Huddle for about four years. At first, Raven was leery about it. She assumed Blair overheard her on the phone talking to Nia about something, and Blair was trying to do reverse psychology on her. When Blair started asking Huddle related questions (and really waiting for responses). Raven answered the same way:

'No, mom, nothing bad happened today."

Blair would say, *'Ray, I didn't ask if anything bad happened. 'Bad' is just a mindset. You change your mindset, you change your day. Is there anything you could have done differently today?"*

Sometimes Raven dreaded these questions because they put her on the spot. That's how life went for an only child. Sometimes her parents would ask certain questions and stare at her until she answered. Khalil was the same — only he made everything into a joke. Once Raven and Khalil realized that Huddle was just about conversation, they both eased up. Mostly she enjoyed Huddle, but it was a long road to get there. Raven was one of those weird teens who enjoyed time with her parents. Sometimes when good things happened during the day, Raven would stop and think, *I can share that for Huddle.*

"So, what is your high from today?" Blair asked.

Raven started off slowly. "Ms. Twizz gave us candy on the bus this morning." Her dad barely listened as he inhaled his food. He chewed with his mouth wide open and made sucking noises with his teeth along the way.

"That's great, Ray," he coughed as he stuffed rice in his mouth. Blair interrupted and told Khalil about the girls dancing at the lake today. Blair was excited and barely let Raven get a word in as she recounted Raven's story to Khalil. Raven tried to fill in the parts as best she could, but her Mom was on a roll. Raven let her do her thing.

"Dirty dancing at the docks, are we now, baby girl?" Khalil snickered as he shuffled food into his mouth and gave her a side eye. The trio burst out laughing.

"No, it wasn't like that, Dad!"

Raven told them both how it felt when something came over her, and she had a hard time sitting still. Raven told them how she was nervous, but when people came and formed a circle around them, she just came alive. Raven even repeated what the woman said to her after the music had gone off: *"You have a gift."* Raven must've talked and talked because her dad stared at her earnestly, and her mom had tears in her eyes. Blair dabbed at her face and said her allergies were acting up.

"Baby girl," her dad whispered. "You do have a gift. The world sees it." Raven fiddled with her food on her plate. She didn't change the subject this time.

"So-" Blair interjected. "What could you have done differently today?" Raven thought for a second and continued playing with her food. She considered the worst parts of her day: her role with her friends, how she met Amir, her continued beef with Taylor. Was Raven making some things bigger than they had to be? Did anything really go wrong today? No, no, it did not.

"I don't think I would change a thing," Raven admitted. Blair and Khalil shared a brief glance.

Khalil breathed, "Me, too, baby girl. That will be my answer for the day, too. In fact, Blair — that is my answer. Next!" He nodded his head at Raven.

"Mom, your turn since you always enjoy putting us on the spot!"

"Yea, Mom, go." Khalil mimicked Raven.

"Ummm." Blair shifted in her seat. "Cocina stopped by the gallery today."

Khalil choked a little. "Is that right?" A vein in his temple bulged.

"Yes"

"I wonder why she didn't come to the station?" Khalil mulled.

"K, why would someone who uses drugs want to go to a police station? Every time she's been there, she's been in handcuffs."

Khalil was quiet. Raven watched this interaction between the two of them. She knew when to take a back seat. "Well, what did she say? She didn't even call my phone," Khalil stopped eating.

Blair moved food around on her plate and avoided Khalil's eyes. "She asked if we could take in Carter."

Raven's interest piqued. Khalil's breathing slowed.

"She said CPS has been knocking, telling her if she doesn't stop with... with the drugs. . . they will take Carter away."

"Blair-" Khalil interrupted.

Blair put her hand up and continued talking,

"Let me finish. Linda, down at the gallery — told us this story about her niece, Shyanne." Blair leaned back in her chair to talk, getting into her story,

"Linda and Shyanne watched a movie, and there was a woman without a baby. Nothing was wrong — the woman simply didn't have children. She went to work, hung out with her friends, and lived her life on her terms. Shyanne didn't understand and kept asking through the whole movie, 'Where is her baby? Where is her baby?' Shyanne continued to quiz Linda and asked, 'Does her friend have a baby?' Linda told us this story, and we laughed and laughed. How funny! Later, I got to really thinking about it. From what Linda has told me about Shyanne and her mom, Shyanne was just living her reality through the movie. In her young life, she had never seen dads or even men with children — she only saw women. She didn't ask where the dads were, just the moms." Blair spoke passionately while Khalil and Raven listened.

"I thought about us," Blair continued. "And Carter. I think he should have experiences too, family experiences. I agree with Cocina, and I think we should take Carter in while she gets herself together. He needs us. They both do." Blair finished with her head held high. Raven's head darted back and forth between her mom and dad. She waited for her dad's reaction while holding her breath. He was quiet while he continued to shuffle food into his mouth.

"I'll tell you what, you teach one art camp for kids over the summer and now you're a social worker, huh?" They all cracked up again, and Raven stopped holding her breath. No matter how tense the situation was, they always shared great laughs. She loved her family for that.

"We'll talk about this later, woman," he said. "Wait, now that I think about it, was that your Huddle? Don't you skate out of Huddle." Khalil retorted.

"Both, I think." Blair was thoughtful. "I think we should take Carter in. That's my high. And what could I do differently? I think we should've done this a long time ago."

"Mmmmm," Khalil grunted.

"Now you go, Mr. Jamison," Blair said.

"You know, slayed a couple dragons today, light work," he looked at Raven and winked again.

"We got free coffee and donuts this morning at Dunkin Donuts."

"Flirting with the ladies and accepting bribes, I see. Isn't that some sort of ethics violation or something?" Blair teased.

"I have to make sure the community is safe," Khalil explained, chuckling.

"Umm, and one thing I could've done differently... I could've ridden to Lake Lacroix where Raven was shaking her tail and put the sirens on." They all fell into a fit of giggles and finished eating dinner. This was her family.

Later that night, Raven cleaned the kitchen and went to her room to shower and get ready for bed. Her bedroom was at the end of the hallway and had a jack and jill bathroom. The other side of her bedroom was their guest room. Most days, it lay empty unless Nana spent the night, but that was rare. Raven wondered if the room would soon be occupied. Raven thought more about her Aunt Cocina and Carter. Aunt Cocina had issues taking care of Carter, and Carter often turned to her dad for help. Carter could walk to the station since he and Aunt Cocina didn't live too far. Blair said Aunt Cocina placed Dad in a lot of unsafe situations when they were young. It must still upset Khalil, and that's why he was so hands-off with Cocina. Either way, Blair reminded him they were family and each other's legacy, so they should help Cocina. Khalil said nothing.

A few months ago, Raven overheard her mom and dad arguing about Carter coming to live with them. Khalil believed Cocina should go to rehab first. Blair agreed, but she believed Carter should come live with them while Cocina went to rehab.

Raven had heard her mom say in a soft voice, *"Raven needs to know her family. She has no other cousins. Blood relatives. It's just us. We need to make this right."* Raven wanted to run in there and scream, *"I'm just fine, Mom! He can come to visit, but he gots to go!"* Only tonight — after dinner, she wasn't so sure she felt the same way anymore. Maybe Raven had been selfish by not wanting her life to change. Cocina was fun when Raven spent time with her. She cursed everyone out, but Raven never saw her with any drugs. Raven didn't know if she had been naïve and missed all the signs, or if she only saw the best in Cocina. Raven felt conflicted.

Carter stayed for a few months a couple years ago, but it didn't last long. Aunt Cocina showed up one afternoon and said she missed her son and was 'better.' She took Carter home and said that she would kick this on her own. Their family had been at odds over it ever since; it was still a touchy subject.

As Raven entered her bedroom, she heard sharp voices. Mom and Dad. They were still downstairs in the kitchen, and Raven could hear them talking through her bathroom.

"Khalil, this is your nephew. He needs us, and you know she's not raising him right," Blair said.

"It's not about raising him, Blair. Cocina is toxic. That's my sister, and I love her, but I'm just not sure about this one, baby. Remember the last time he stayed for a couple weeks? Cocina called all hours of the night, came by at midnight to drop off his lunchbox. Signed him out of school that one day talking about she was taking him to get ice cream. Do you know how embarrassing that shit is? My own station being called to go search for my sister and nephew! And they find them at a Dairy Queen three towns over?! I'm sorry, Blair. . . I like the life we've created — matter of fact!" Khalil's voice rose even louder. Raven had not heard him this upset in a while. "We don't even know who Carter's dad is. Cocina has told no one if she even knows. What are we supposed to do with that? Blair, what?"

The silence was deafening, and it made Raven nervous.

She showered and settled into bed. She was just about ready to shut off the light when she heard a knock at the front door. Blair and Khalil's bedroom were downstairs, at the back of the house, and they would get to the door before she would. Raven looked at her cell phone: Eleven-fifteen. It was kind of late. Raven threw the blanket back and stood at the top of the steps in her robe and slippers. Her hair was still wet from the shower. She tightened her robe around her waist. Someone banged on the door a second time, this time louder and more forceful. Whoever it was behind the door wanted their attention.

Khalil looked over his shoulder at Raven standing at the top of the steps. He gave her a weak smile before he opened the door. He also had on his robe, and man flops. Blair stood off to the back, by the kitchen. With the door wide open, there stood Carter with a few trash bags, a scowl, and an older White lady with a clipboard. They were standing on Blair's 'Check yo' energy' doormat.

"Mr. and Mrs. Jamison?" the White woman didn't look up from her clipboard addressing them.

Khalil and Blair nodded their heads.

"I'm Ms. Cottman, from DCFS," she said, popping gum in her mouth. "Ms. Cocina Jamison listed you as the first placement choice for Carter."

"Excuse me?"

"Let me start over, I apologize. The State of Louisiana had to take custody of Mr. Carter Jamison here because of concerns with Ms. Jamison's parenting abilities. We asked if she had any biological family that Carter could stay with, and if not, he would have to be placed in foster care. She indicated that you could take him in. I apologize that I could not call. We had some issues getting Carter out of the home, and I lost my cell phone." Ms. Cottman continued looking at her clipboard and popped gum in her mouth. Khalil noticed the police officers standing behind Ms. Cottman. His colleagues.

"So, are you able to take him?"

"Uhh yes, yes, of course." Blair nodded and stepped out from beyond the kitchen. She tightened her own robe around her waist.

Khalil stood frozen in silence.

"Of course, Carter, come in here, honey." Blair stepped from the shadows.

Carter shuffled into the house with a grimace on his face, dragging in his trash bags. Raven stood motionless at the top of the steps, watching this encounter unfold in front of her. It all happened so fast. Raven wanted to scream,

"No, no, we can't take him. We didn't even have time to finish talking about it yet. There had to be other options."

"I'll bring the rest of his things tomorrow, and I'll be back to discuss the details, housing requirements, and answer any questions that you may have." Ms. Cottman handed Khalil a yellow piece of paper.

Khalil read the paper, already knowing what it said. He was familiar with DCFS forms. He had helped serve this kind of paper many times at the station. Khalil looked behind Ms. Cottman at the officers. They nodded their heads at Khalil out of respect before they turned away and escorted Ms. Cottman to her car. The officers and Ms. Cottman shared a laugh at something only they heard.

Khalil's jaw tightened. All hell broke loose in one day

CHAPTER 6

Carter

Carter woke up in a new house, his Uncle Lil's house. One week went by, then two, then three. September rolled in, and the seasons changed; the air cooled down. The sweet smell of the oak trees turned musky. The air wasn't so thick with the stench of fish from Lake Lacroix. In a quaint house on Sycamore Street, there was a cancer festering. It was getting bigger and bigger and more dangerous and confusing by the minute. It infected everyone in the home differently.

It was Carter, and he knew it.

There are too many damn candles around here, he thought. He could smell them everywhere. In his own room, which he thought was way too big, Aunt B had put those funny smelling plugins in the wall, just adding to the smells. When the air clicked on, the vents even wafted out something fruity — he coughed, waking up. *These people were crazy.*

Carter pulled his mattress onto the floor, and it hit the hardwood with a loud thud. He snatched the plugin out of the wall and threw it across the room. He found a pen on the floor and jabbed it into the sockets until the casing came loose from the wall. Carter opened his window and pulled out the screen. He drew the curtains closed again, so it was dark.

She was gone again, and Carter wondered how long this time. He could make it two weeks, that was the longest time she stayed gone before. Aunt B cooked and cleaned all day long, which was a good thing. He already stashed cookies, crackers, half-eaten nuggets, and sunflower seeds in the sock drawer. He made sure to visit the refrigerator every night once everyone went to sleep. That way, no one would know it was him. Carter contemplated putting some food in Uncle Lil's garage, just in case.

Carter's bedroom door opened, and Aunt B rushed in, tripping on the corner of Carter's mattress on the floor. Carter squinted up at her and noticed fruit flies buzzing around her head. Her eyes bugged out once she saw them too.

"Ahhhh," she yelped. Aunt B ran out of the room, and before Carter could do anything, she was back with a can of Lysol. Carter lay there watching in amusement while she shrieked and sprayed the can around her head.

"Honey, you don't have to take the food. Everything here is yours to keep. You don't have to even ask," Aunt B coughed while talking. She stuck her head out of the window and snorted. The Lysol burned at Carter's eyes.

"Where is the window screen?" Blair stuck her head back in the room and looked around.

Carter eyed the screen he stuffed in the closet minutes earlier. She followed his eyes, and hers squinted when she found the screen. She inhaled.

"Carter. You cannot keep food in your room. And you cannot take the window screen out. It's not safe."

Aunt B had taken a leave of absence from the gallery and was always in Carter's face these days. Ms. Cottman came the week before to meet with everyone, and she suggested it.

Carter's arms began to twitch on the mattress under the blanket, he didn't like her standing over top of him. *What if she took my food? Or stepped on me?* Carter mused.

He leapt to his feet and threw the plugins at Aunt B that he just pulled out of the walls. His ragged breath intensified, and he tossed everything off his dresser with one swift motion. His eyes pulsed out of his head, and he felt heat throughout his body. He didn't know what she was going to do, but he had to be ready. Carter eyed the cellphone Ms. Cottman gave him a few weeks ago, sitting in the corner of the room. He never used it, there was no one for him to call. Ms. Cottman was just as bad as Twelve, and she was probably tracking the phone. Carter knew it was his only option, so he knelt, grabbed the phone, and darted out of the room. Aunt B screamed behind him as he ran through the house.

Where was She exactly? She, being his Mom. Ms. Cottman wouldn't give him location details. He didn't see the signs this time; wasn't able to prepare. Carter hadn't talked to her since the night he showed up on Uncle Lil's doorstep. Uncle Lil was cool, but he could not stay there with Aunt B policing his every move and Raven watching him like he was wounded or something.

Carter sat hunched in the corner of the laundry room. He scrolled to Ms. Cottman's name in his phone. He found her contact and sent her a text message.

Carter: *I can't stay here. I'm guna leave. call me.*

CHAPTER 7

"He needs space. Time," Ms. Cottman explained to Khalil and Blair.

"He hasn't said a word, though," Blair challenged.

"That can be normal, he's been through some trauma. There are a lot of things we still don't know."

"And his dad?" Khalil stood in a corner off by himself.

With a sigh, Ms. Cottman says, "We still don't know who that is."

"Mmmmm . ." Khalil grunted. "And where exactly is Cocina?"

"Right now, she's in rehab in Mississippi. It will be at least four weeks before they allow her to contact anyone. Please understand that this time is serious. She injured a few officers when they tried to get Carter out of the home. We don't think the judge will be as lenient this time, returning custody to her. She has to at least finish four weeks. At least."

Khalil shifted his weight and snorted.

Phoenix, Khalil, Blair, Raven, sat in the living room with Ms. Cottman, having a one-sided conversation. Ms. Cottman had no information to share, but she wanted them to do a million things. Carter wasn't home from school yet, and Ms. Cottman stopped by unannounced before they left for the Voodoo Festival that night.

"He needs to know you're with him every step of the way. Remember, he's had no stability and has moved four times in the past six months. He hasn't been in school consistently more than a few weeks at a time. It's a marathon, not a sprint." Ms. Cottman continued. "In the meantime. Here are some phone numbers for Carter. He needs therapy, and these are a list of counselors accepting new patients."

Ms. Cottman peered around the room, her eyes stopping at dirt on the floor. Three nights before, Carter ripped up Blair's beloved plants and tossed dirt everywhere. He took one of Khalil's grilling forks and poked Blair's pillar candles she lit every night for dinner. Khalil thought they cleaned it all up, but he noticed Ms. Cottman checking out the dirt.

He shouted, "I had to put him in a damn safety hold like at work."

Khalil walked into the kitchen and grabbed the broom. He needed something to steady his nervous hands. He thought about Carter and how long it took him to relax in Khalil's arms while he was being held down with the fork in his hand. Khalil wouldn't let go while Carter glared at Blair. The next day, Khalil worked overtime at the station. Some nights, he made it home just as the table was being set. It was always "some big thing" happening in Lake Lacroix that he needed to tend to. Funny, there never seemed to be so many criminals and missing persons in Lake Lacroix until after Carter moved in. Khalil's jokes became less frequent. His dances were less animated until there were no dances.

Phoenix came over every day. She and Blair worked together and came up with a schedule, so they never left Carter alone. Phoenix always remained positive. "*Carter will be okay. And Cocina! She's the strongest out of all of us. She just needs time.*"

Phoenix brought food and clothes for Carter. Raven couldn't remember a time when Nana cooked more than potato salad. That was Nana's signature contribution and the one thing she could make — potato salad. But here she was, cooking for Carter and the family. Truth be told, Nana struggled with her own feelings of guilt, and it was one she couldn't escape. When she looked in Carter's eyes, she saw sadness.

Brushing dirt into the trash can, Khalil stewed... *This is Phoenix's fault.* He and his mom were never close, but now with history repeating itself, DCFS entered their lives like a thief in the night, and he wanted to argue. It festered and churned in his stomach, waiting to be unleashed. Phoenix felt Khalil's anger festering towards her. The notion enveloped Khalil like smoke as he remembered Phoenix's indifference when he was younger. Letting go of that hurt would be the most arduous task for Khalil. He felt out of control. His house was in turmoil, and his anger blocked his thoughts. And while his wife was committed to Carter's healing to alleviate the trauma, Khalil's own healing lay swept under a rug that was pulled out from under him. Khalil had told no one that he had been calling Cocina over and over. He called her cell phone until it would stop ringing, and it would just beep. They said she was in rehab, but he had to know for himself, for sure.

Raven sat in the living room frozen in place. She didn't know what to say, so she said nothing. She was sorry that her mom went into Carter's room and touched anything, and she was even more sorry that she had helped — but she just hated to see her throwing buckets of water on the fire that was Carter, so she helped her mom clean.

It only took three days when they noticed the food. Carter was hiding food. They couldn't figure it out at first. The family would go to sleep at night, and they would wake up to the refrigerator ransacked and things missing. They had found moldy chicken nuggets in his pillowcases. Half-filled juice bottles stuffed under his bed. Ketchup stains on the wall. Mayonnaise, salad dressing, old roast beef, fruit. They would mysteriously disappear. When they explained to Carter that he could have anything he wanted to eat, he went into his room and stayed there the rest of the night; he didn't even come down to eat. Blair, Khalil, and Raven Huddled about it that night over the dinner table.

He scribbled into notebooks. Dozens of different notebooks. He would sit in his room just scribbling. The words never made sense, but again if you touched them, his eyes would stone you.

There were also sleep issues. He never seemed to get a full night's rest. He usually went to sleep early into the next morning, but he kept the TV volume blasted all night. When they tried to turn the TV down, he got upset. The next day he would be irritable at school and lash out because he was tired. They finally compromised and put the TV down low enough so the rest of the family could get some sleep without hearing his programs. This cycle continued and continued.

Raven wondered how long they could go on like this. Her mom playing a Stepford Wife and her dad missing in action most days. Carter grunted and pointed to things. Other times Raven would find him just staring off in space or scowling. The only thing he enjoyed — and Raven meant thoroughly enjoyed — was watching Mukbang videos on YouTube. Raven made the mistake of turning it off one day, and Carter swung his head around and glared at her so hard she was sure he had pulled a neck muscle.

“Give him time,” Ms. Cottman said, putting on her coat. Raven wasn’t sure time was on their side.

Just then, Carter opened the front door and walked into the living room.

“Hi Carter,” Ms. Cottman said flatly.

Carter looked her up and down and then at each person in the room.

“Mrs. Jamison, give me an update in a few days,” Ms. Cottman nodded, slinking out of the house. Her lips were pursed, watching Carter. He moved into the kitchen and stuffed water bottles in his bag.

Shutting the door behind Ms. Cottman, Blair clapped her hands together, “Ok, let’s get ready. Carter, I laid your costume out on the bed. I thought you might like to be a police officer, like Uncle Lil,” Blair suggested.

Carter’s eyes widened, and he turned on his heel as the doorbell sang.

“Thanks, Carter.”

He waved his hand over his head at Trinity as he shut the door behind her and walked upstairs.

“Hey, Brown Girl! You ready?” Trinity carried a bag of costume clothes.

Raven didn’t answer but watched Carter get to the end of the hallway and shut his door. About an hour later, the entire family stood together. It was a late October night as they headed to the annual Voodoo Festival. Before Carter came to live with them, Raven had invited Trinity, her festival buddy. Amir was coming this year too, he informed her earlier during lunch. When Raven accepted his follow request on Instagram, it became easier to talk to him. Nana left and went to pick up Johnny Gil, and he knocked on Carter's door for a full five minutes before Carter came out without his costume. No one said anything to him about it.

Nana was dressed as a nightstand, and she wore a small lampshade around her waist. Johnny Gil painted the number 1 on his shirt. He still had on khaki pants and loafers. That was their costume. Yikes.

Trinity and Raven painted their faces in her room and dotted black freckles on their noses and cheeks. They did their makeup; Trinity chose a black lip, and up against her already rich skin tone, it looked dark and mysterious. Raven went for bright red. The hues played against her freckles and pink cheeks. Both girls put their hair in puffs at the sides of their heads; they were Minnie Mouse. Blair and Khalil inserted Black power into everything they did. They were dressed as Play and Sharane from *House Party*.

The Voodoo Festival was held thirty minutes away in NOLA at a large park. Raven reminisced at how much she loved

Louisiana this time of year. She didn't need a jacket yet, and the sky was a pretty shade of burnt orange around dusk. Tonight, the South was out. Raven glimpsed everyone around her. Amir's hand brushed up against Raven's when they walked; he was dressed as Black Panther. Trinity whispered in the car that she was taking one for the team, and it was her turn to be the third wheel. Raven reminded her that this was not a date, so technically, she wasn't the third wheel.

People of all colors, ages, and sizes moved around freely, eating, and drinking over the large open fields. Oak trees lined the skies around them, and a breeze from Lake Lacroix whipped through every few seconds. Somewhere someone barbequed, and the scent tickled Raven's nose. The same cars Raven saw each week at the car wash at home were posted up too. They had different colored lights in the doors and wheels. Their owners stood in front of their cars, proud. Music rang out as people did the *"Cha Cha Slide"* around her. The beat called to Raven, and within minutes, she was doing the dance in dramatic fashion. She swung her hips and shimmied. Her light pink highlighter sparkled under the festival lights. Amir cheered her on from the side, and Nana danced next to Raven. Johnny Gil awkwardly moved next to Nana. Trinity and Blair both had their phones out, recording. Blair recorded Raven, and Trinity recorded Johnny Gil. Khalil slid next to Raven and started grooving too. Trinity nudged Raven, and she motioned to Carter. Raven watched Carter walking off to the side of her mom and dad. His hands were deep in his jean pockets, and his hood was up. He didn't want to dress up. Raven told her mom that, but Blair bought the costume anyway.

Carter eyed the food trucks. He ran his finger against the hot glass of the pretzel stand. He peered at the popcorn and lingered in front of the cotton candy. He squinted his eyes at the hotdogs.

“Dad,” Raven slowed down. “I think Carter wants something to eat.” Khalil looked at Carter and shouted over the music,

“Do you want something to eat?”

Carter nodded his head yes.

“Which one do you want?” Khalil asked. He walked to Carter and took his wallet out of his pocket. Carter pointed to everything Raven saw him looking at. Popcorn, hot dogs, and cotton candy. He also pointed at the candy apples.

Khalil bought it all for Carter and his eyes danced with wonder every time the food was placed in his hands. He struggled trying to carry everything, and Raven took the popcorn box from him.

“I'll take one,” she offered.

Carter snatched it back and grimaced at her; he wanted to carry all his food. . . himself. Carter looked around, finding an empty picnic table. He sat down and began eating. With precision, he ate the whole box of popcorn, then he ate the full bag cotton candy. Blair knew he would be thirsty because she walked to another food truck and bought him a lemonade. By the time she got back with the large yellow cup, Carter was settling in on the jumbo hot dog, and finally, he ate the entire candy apple down to the core.

The group watched Carter. He shoveled food into his mouth like he wouldn't eat again like he had to consume it, or he would regret it later. Someone walked by and stared at Carter, woofing food into his mouth. Khalil sat down at the picnic table with Carter and peered back at the person staring at Carter. He kept walking.

Amir whispered to Raven, “This looks like a family thing, I’m gonna head out.” he shook his head.

Raven swallowed. She didn't want him to leave, but she didn't want him to see this. Whatever this was. Raven nodded at Amir.

Carter was still for a few minutes, pausing to take long gulps from his lemonade.

“Do you want anything else?” Khalil asked.

Screams bellowed from the crowd as voices rapped into the mic. Whoever was on stage had police lights as part of their act. Carter’s arm twitched as he turned to shake his head at

Uncle Lil. His stomach churned, and he vomited right there. A sea of pink and purple matter, popcorn kernels, and hot dog bits lay in front of Khalil's feet.

Raven jumped back. She glimpsed Carter's eyes when the music echoed from the speakers, fear. She saw fear. Watching Carter vomit, she knew they had something in common. Anxiety.

CHAPTER 8

Carter

Carter sat in the library at Lake Lacroix Elementary School. He was kicked out of class for stealing bookoo milk cartons. He needed to add them to his collection under the bed.

"One, two, three," he counted around the classroom. Three extra cartons. Perfect. Once the other students each took one, Carter placed the rest in his book bag to take home. Mrs. Johnson, the school Principal, pulled him out of class just as he zipped his bag. She spoke into a walkie talkie, "I found him. Jamison. Yes. Get me a parent," she sneered.

She was on her bullshit too. They had already moved him into a self-contained class, and now they tried to make him stay there all day. *All day?* Carter didn't think so. Days later, security chased Carter through the halls, two in one hallway — and two in another. Carter ran laps down the lengthy corridors, daring them to chase him. He was slightly amused at the whole thing. Now, Mrs. Johnson made Carter sit in the library until someone came to pick him up. The loud fire alarm at the school sounded, interrupting Carter's thoughts.

"Get moving!" the old Librarian yelled.

Carter's stomach began to hurt, and his arms twitched. *What the hell was that noise? And why?* The noise intensified, and so did Carter's breathing. He jumped up, prepared to run, smacking into the librarian. She tripped back, and her glasses flung up on her face. Carter darted out of the library and searched around the busy hallway for an exit. Before he could move, Mrs. Johnson intercepted him for the second time that day.

"My office now!" she screamed.

Security surrounded Carter and carried him into Mrs. Johnson's office, kicking and screaming. Mrs. Johnson didn't even close her office door when she called Uncle Lil. Carter watched spit fly from her lips when she spoke, and with an *uh-huh, uh-huh,* here and there — she twisted the knife a little deeper. "We're exasperated. If his behaviors don't improve, we'll be forced to send him to the alternative school — we just can't manage him," she told Khalil. The police arrived at the school the same time Uncle Lil got there. He looked at them and looked at Carter. His face was blank. "Let's go," he motioned. Carter's shoulders hung low as they rode home in silence.

Later that night, they sat at the table for dinner. Aunt B insisted on cooking every single night; they never ordered pizza. This became the worst part of Carter's day. They wanted to talk while they ate, and it was awkward. Carter had trouble chewing, looking up, and talking at the same time. They had all these different things to talk about every day, and he wasn't sure he had anything they'd like to hear. Last week, before they moved him to the self-contained class. Carter sat next to Bryce, Raven's friend's brother, at lunch. He was drawing a picture. Not like a coloring book picture, a real picture, he drew himself with the brightest coloring pencils Carter ever saw. Carter thought he could talk about that one night but decided against it. He wasn't ready for the conversation that might come afterwards.

He thought about dinner the night before; it was a tense one. Nana was there cooking, and she accidently burnt up the pot roast. Aunt B was helping her, and the rest of the family sat at the table waiting for the food to be brought out. *"I'm gonna call Johnny Gil and have him swing by the Walmart and buy some chicken, I burnt this one up."* Nana sighed.

Carter studied the roast. It was shriveled up and a dark shade of black. The potatoes and carrots sat around the roast, caramelized and hardened. There was no juice or gravy, it all dried up in the oven. Carter knew any other night, Uncle Lil would have made fun of Nana for burning up the food, but tonight no one laughed.

"It's fine Nana, we have some leftover chicken from last night, we can warm that up," Aunt B rubbed Nana's back.

Nana took the entire roast and tossed it in the trash can. Carter's eyes widened. Khalil just took out the trash, so the can was empty when the roast hit the bottom with a hard thud. The carrots and potatoes splattered around it. Nana went to the refrigerator and searched for the other chicken they had for dinner from the previous night.

Carter winced, thinking of how much meat would be wasted. If he had felt like talking, he would cuss them out tonight. He started to yell, but the words caught in his throat. Instead, he stood and, without saying a word, slid in behind Nana. He retrieved the roast from the trash can with his bare hands.

"No honey don't eat that, I burned it up," Nana said, as she tried to take the roast from Carter. He pulled away from Nana and walked back to his seat with the roast in hand. He left a trail of juice on the floor as hot fluid ran down his hands and arms. Carter placed the entire roast on his plate, cut into the middle of it where it had not been burned, and ate from it, right then and there. He didn't eat any sides, just the meat. *Besides*, Carter weighed. *He had chicken all the time.* He hadn't had roast beef in years.

Carter avoided everyone's eyes as they stared at him. No one dared say a word. Nana looked shocked and partly amused that despite her ruined roast, someone was still eating it. Aunt B stood and warmed up the chicken from the night before. The rest of the family sat there: Raven, Blair, Khalil, and Nana eating chicken- and Carter eating roast beef. If anyone had come to the house, they would have thought the family was crazy. Gravy on the floor, roast beef, and chicken all over the table.

CHAPTER 9

"What did you get for answer 3?" Amir asked.

Raven was deep in thought in chemistry class.

"Oh, um, 4.75."

Raven and Amir were going over numbers preparing for their project. "What are you over there thinking about?"

"A lot on my mind. This thing with Carter is a mess," Raven admitted.

Raven wanted to tell her mom about Amir and about their friendship. Blair always listened intently, but she was so preoccupied with Carter these days that Raven never got around to telling her.

"What's up with the therapist? I thought he was supposed to see someone?" said Amir.

"I don't know. They told my mom there was a waiting list, and they would call in a few days. It's been weeks. . . What did you get for number 8?" Raven changed the subject.

Amir cut his eyes at her. "Uh, 7.3."

"We have midterms in two weeks, and I still cannot figure this sequencing out," Raven grumbled.

"You know I can help you. Numbers are my game," Amir quipped.

Raven smiled as the bell rang, and they headed to lunch. Raven went through the motions of eating, distracted the entire time. Carter and her parents consumed her thoughts. She tried to brush them out of her mind, but it was easier said than done.

Before she knew it, the lunch bell rang, and students spilled into the hallway. Entering the gym, it resembled Essence Fest during 4th of July weekend — Black people everywhere. Their school was predominately black, and white students were the minority. The gym was sectioned off, and students lined up according to their last name, so Raven knew they were making teams for volleyball. Good. Raven was a beast in volleyball.

The year before, they played volleyball, and Taylor and Raven were on opposing sides. Raven spiked the ball, and it narrowly whizzed by Taylor's head. She moved just in time, otherwise, it was coming straight at her face. Taylor had looked at Raven with death in her eyes. Raven tried to explain it wasn't intentional, but she didn't really have a chance to talk because the game continued.

Raven searched for the "J" section to get in line as she heard her name being called over the gym teacher's walkie talkie.

"Please have Raven Jamison report to room B103."

"Raveeen Jamisonnnn," her gym teacher screamed into the microphone. "I heard!" Raven yelled, gathering her book bag. She headed towards the door with everyone watching. Raven hung her head and walked out, cutting her eyes at her gym teacher.

B103, B103 ... Raven couldn't remember where B103 was located, but it sounded familiar. She glanced at the school map in her agenda and saw that B103 was near the nurse's office. She couldn't figure out why she was being pulled out of class, and she was slightly irritated she would miss volleyball. Raven headed in that direction of B103 and saw Ms. Whitaker, the school counselor, standing outside of the door waving at her.

Her walking slowed.

She forgot Blair signed her up for counseling last year regarding her anxiety and where it came from. October of last year, Blair saw Raven in her bathroom crying. Raven didn't know what she was crying about, really. Raven was on her cycle, and to her — that was answer enough. But to Blair, it was ammunition because the next thing Raven knew, Ms. Whitaker was calling her to her office once a week at her mom's insistence for group therapy with a bunch of other girls who got sent up the river by their snitching parents. She made a mental note to tell her mom she wanted out of that group.

Ms. Whitaker was young. She looked about 25. She wore different color eyeglasses and bright colored lipstick every day. She had the darkest, smoothest Black skin that Raven had ever seen, and up against the bright colors she wore, she stood out when she walked into a room. Unfortunately, when she strolled in, she did so to look for one of us girls from the group and would come right up and talk there in front of everyone. If Raven weren't so busy hiding from her, Raven would admire her style and personality.

"Ms. Raven, I've missed you! Come sit down here, I have your favorite chair! We have to catch up. I know some of us probably had an eventful summer!"

Ms. Whitaker shot questions at Raven straight away, and instantly she had a headache. Raven liked Ms. Whitaker. She was nice and always seemed to recognize what she was thinking. She turned everything into a story; she therapized them. It wasn't bad, and some topics were interesting. Last year they made these "calm down" jars with slime and glue. They looked like homemade lava lamps, and the girls loved making them. Raven pushed those thoughts out of her head. She was ready to play volleyball. Not see Ms. Whitaker.

Raven had to be mature as she remembered the things, she disliked about group therapy. One session last year, Raven was the last one to leave from Ms. Whitaker's office. Ms. Whitaker left to go to the bathroom, and Raven forgot her notebook and ran back to get it. Her book bag was next to Ms. Whitaker's desk, and when she bent to pick it up, she glimpsed her name. Raven wasn't even looking when she saw it, but it was right there on a notepad.

Ms. Whitaker had written, *Raven Jamison — poor self-expression.* What the heck did that mean? Poor self-expression? Raven told no one what she saw, but she knew how Ms. Whitaker felt. Thanks to her own words.

Ms. Whitaker's office was bright and full of colors and pictures. She had photos of Barack Obama, Beyonce, LeBron James, Yara Shahidi, Nipsey Hussle, Cardi B, Prince Harry, Meghan Markle, Solange, Kamala Harris, John Lewis, Kobe Bryant, Sean King, H.E.R, Kevin Hart, Will Smith, Issa Rae, Michael B. Jordan, Tamika Mallory, Zendaya. Her cement walls were littered with Black and brown faces and a few Caucasian ones down for the cause. The faces covered the space in a beautiful mosaic of Melanin. Big pictures, small pictures, some overlapping others; close enough to create a collage, but still bold enough to stand on their own. The ceiling lights illuminated each of the faces, smiling and posing back at Raven. There were rugs and large beanbags. Her face softened, and she unclenched her fists. The office calmed

Raven. That she couldn't deny. Raven stepped inside and noticed that they were alone.

"Where is the group?" Raven asked.

"I'm meeting with everyone alone for the first couple of sessions. Then we'll start the group back up. *"It was a setup. I was in here alone so she could pelt me with questions and then write things down to read later*, she figured. She wouldn't get Raven this time.

"I'm not really interested this year Ms. Whitaker. Can you call my mom and tell her I don't want to be in the group any longer?"

"Oh?" Ms. Whitaker raised an eyebrow. Shock registered across her face as she studied Raven over the top of her glasses sitting on her nose. "Well, let's start slow, tell me about your summer," she leaned back in her bean bag chair.

Raven's brief show of making a stand quickly dissipated as she played with her earrings and twirled her curls. She glanced at the clock until six minutes had passed, but it seemed like an hour. Ms. Whitaker had a stress ball on her desk, and before Raven knew it, she grabbed the ball and began squeezing it to busy herself.

The summer flashed in Raven's mind. The heat, the bugs, the lake. Raven and the girls had spent hours and hours dancing, talking, and listening to music at each other's houses.

Raven and her family went on vacation to California for one week before school had started. Raven thought California was absolutely beautiful. They'd vacationed before, but this time was different. Usually, her Mom wanted to explore every nook and cranny of a new place, but this time they spent long days at the beach.

"Dad complained about the heat, which was funny because we live in Louisiana where it's scorching hot all the time anyway, but he claimed California was too hot." Raven's eyes sparkled.

Ms. Whitaker leaned forward in her seat.

"Not Mr. Khalil!" she chuckled. She knew Raven's Dad and thought he was funny. He often came to the school doing "Coffee with a Cop" events, and everyone at school called him "Mr. Khalil." Raven explained to Ms. Whitaker how everyone in California seemed so cool and easygoing. Everything appeared fun. Blair enjoyed California but went on and on about the privilege she saw everywhere in California.

"Look at these houses, look! Why would someone need all the space? There are too many places to disappear. You know how you know you're in a good neighborhood? You see White people running and exercising. There's a coffee shop and juice bar on every corner. I bet you their property taxes are sky high. Gentrification everywhere. That's how you know." Blair

explained. Raven didn't even know what property taxes and gentrification were, but the way her mom talked about it, she knew it was something she wanted no parts from.

Raven didn't care about the houses or neighborhoods. She looked at the girls and the way they were dressed. In California, the girls wore crop tops, tights, and their hair flowed in the wind. Raven told Ms. Whitaker she decided she's going to change her look and become more of herself, whoever that may be. Raven described her style this year as just comfortable. College was soon approaching, and she didn't want to be the Vans wearing girl anymore; she uncrossed her feet and displayed her new AirMax's. She was an AirMax girl now.

It was a step.

Raven showed Ms. Whitaker her "Be You" necklace that they got from a crafter at Venice Beach. It felt as if she was trying to convince Ms. Whitaker that she was "fixed" enough to be dropped from group therapy, but as she continued talking, it felt good to let it out. There were so many things to process with her. Maybe she would make a list for next time. She told Ms. Whitaker how she begged her parents to let her get her palm read by a Gypsy on the boardwalk. They finally agreed, and Raven could barely contain her excitement. Raven had seen it a few times on *American Horror Story,* so she knew she had to sit real still and get serious. Raven did all those things and let the

Gypsy lady do her thing. She was an older White woman wearing a ton of beads and scarves around her neck and head. Her nails were painted bright red, and she had on thick eyeliner and tons of mascara. The woman drew on her eyebrows and lined her lips with dark brown liner. Raven didn't see a crystal ball. She was exactly what Raven had envisioned. She touched Raven's hands a few times before flipping them over and examining Raven's palms and the tops of her hands.

"Umph," the woman said at random moments.

Blair and Khalil stood off to the side, her dad half amused, and her mom half concerned.

"Mmmmmm child," the psychic swayed. *"You will be growing up soon."*

Raven knew that already. *Tell me something I don't know,* Raven thought. The woman repeated, *"You will be growing up soon, you will be growing up soon."*

She began rocking back and forth and circling her pointer finger in Raven's hand. She stopped circling her finger and lightly patted the center of Raven's hand.

"You'll heal them all," the woman said, tapping Raven's hand once more. She pushed back in her seat and said, *"Done, come get her,"* nodding to Raven's parents. Blair rushed over and whisked Raven away while Khalil jokingly asked the woman for a refund.

"Umph," the woman grunted to Khalil, swatting him away.

"You will be growing up soon, and you'll heal them all? What did that even mean?" Raven separated the two sentences, and then she put them together. Any which way she put them, it still made little sense. Raven explained this to Ms. Whitaker as she intently listened, her fist tucked under her hand. Ms. Whitaker kept pushing her large glasses up over her nose. She pensively spoke, "Well, do you have any thoughts about what she meant by that statement? It seems to me we could take those sentences any kind of way. It's all based on your perception of the situation."

"I already know I'm going to grow up soon. We'll be in college soon enough. It's the second sentence that I questioned," Raven pondered.

"That's interesting. We'll have to write this down and note the date so we can come back to it in December, and you can start your *Who I Am* project with that information."

Great, Raven thought. *Here we go — another project.* At the end of the semester, every therapy group has to do a *Who I Am vs Who I Was* project. They were given large poster boards and magazines to cut. They made a collage of different things they were interested in at the time and who they see themselves as currently. Raven did it last year, and it was cool to see what was on her mind that many months ago versus what she was preoccupied with now. Raven added Ms. Whitaker's project to the list along with her chemistry project. Eleventh grade was starting to feel crowded.

Ms. Whitaker and Raven continued talking until the bell rang. She rushed to gather her things, not realizing how much time had passed.

"Ms. Raven, do you still want me to call Mom and ask her to pull you out of the group?"

Raven paused in the doorway. Her stomach wasn't in knots anymore. Maybe there is something to this talking thing; one more year couldn't hurt.

"No, you don't have to call her," Raven replied.

"Sounds good to me." Ms. Whitaker held the door for Raven with a smile.

The next two periods, Raven focused on her schoolwork, trying to block everything out of her mind. Raven got excellent grades, especially in English class. For some reason, the words and scenes unfolded before her and took Raven to another world. Her English class was reading *The Crucible*, and she needed another world right now. Unfortunately, English class also meant words had to be read out loud, in the presence of people, and that's the part she hated; people staring at her while she read. Raven snapped out of her thoughts when the last bell rang as they were dismissed for the day.

CHAPTER 10

When Raven got off the bus, she saw her mom's car. Blair was in the kitchen cooking, and Raven immediately smelled the warm scent of garlic. "Mmm, what are you cooking?"

"Steak and potatoes," Blair beamed. "How was your day, baby girl?"

Raven held that question a second too long. She remembered nicer times when Blair would ask her that same question, and they would talk and talk. These days, Raven knew the question would be followed with something Carter related. Raven didn't want it to, not just yet. She just wanted to talk to her mom about *her* day and nothing else.

"It was good," Raven started. "Let me tell you about this chemistry project we have to do . . ." beginning the horror story.

"Oh, Ray, do you know a girl named Taylor?" Blair interrupted. Raven stopped dead in her tracks. This couldn't be good. Raven looked around the kitchen and noted Blair's work bag out, and the contents were strewn about on the table. Pictures of buildings, words, and business cards littered the table.

French. The word French was written on the business cards. Only Raven knew this wasn't in reference to the country.

"Yes, I know her. Why?"

"Okay, good, she and her family are coming over for supper tonight."

She couldn't be serious right now.

"Mom! I've told you a million times about her. The girl from the dance team? The one who hasn't liked me since eighth grade?"

"Wow, baby girl. I didn't know that was her. I'm so sorry."

"Are you serious right now? Why would you do this!?" Raven cried.

"Her mom is a doctor. The gallery just secured her account to do her marketing and branding. I invited her and her family over for dinner tonight."

Raven groaned again. More of a scream. Who was this person she was even talking to right now? Her mom already knew how she felt about Taylor. This wasn't happening.

"She hates me, Mom!"

"I'm so sorry, Ray. I really dropped the ball with this one. The gallery asked me to take it even though I'm on leave. We really need the account."

Raven's head started hurting. She heard her mom's words, but they weren't landing. How had this happened, the one person she didn't get along with, now in a few brief hours, would be in her home, breaking bread with her? She wondered if Blair did this purposely to teach her a lesson of some sort. That idea sounded crazy to Raven, she knew her mom wouldn't do that to her, but still — she needed answers, and this wasn't adding up. Raven was trying to be the mature one. Had tried to hold it together just like she watched her Mom do so many times, but this was too much. Raven didn't even have time to process things, it was just sprung on her.

"This is Carter's fault," Raven said out loud.

Blair stopped stirring the food and turned towards Raven. "Now you know that's not true either, Ray, stop that." Blair's voice was a little sterner.

"It is his fault," Raven screamed. "You wouldn't have forgotten about Taylor if *he* wasn't here. You forget about everything now! And Dad's never home! And now I have to sit with *her* for dinner, all because Carter is here! And where is he anyway, holed up in his room, right?!" Raven stopped to get her breath. Hot, angry tears rolled from Raven's eyes as her words spewed. Blair turned off the food at the stove and walked right up to Raven. Blair stood there, face to face, nose to nose with her daughter. Raven studied her mom, Blair's red locs framing her face. Her nose was wet with a light dab of sweat.

"You better watch yourself, Raven. Watch how you talk to me. I know this is hard. I get it, and I hear you. I'm so sorry about today, I honestly forgot about Taylor, and that is my fault. Carter is not here; he is out with Nana. I asked Nana to take him, so there were no . . . uh . . . Mishaps. I'm doing the best that I can, and I know you are too. But watch the way you talk to me. Okay?" Blair flatly whispered to Raven.

"Yes, mom," Raven muttered. Tears still ran down her cheeks. Raven sharply turned away from her mom and ran up to her bedroom.

Blair was glad Raven had turned away when she did. She didn't want Raven to see tears forming in her own eyes. She turned the food back on and began stirring, now with shaky hands.

Upstairs, Raven cried into her pillow. Blair expressed many times she was building her brand and needed to make sure her customers felt like family. Blair loved the gallery. She often had clients over for meals, and Raven sat through boring dinner talk about textiles, framing, mounting, and other things art related.

This one would be the most painful, though.

Raven grabbed her phone and called Jasmine; she would know just how to handle Taylor. As Raven called, a text message came through on Raven's cell phone.

Blair: *They'll be here at 6.*

Raven swiped it away. . . and Jasmine didn't answer her call. Raven's hands fell into her lap, phone still in hand. She knew she would have to go at this one alone tonight. No friends, and apparently no family. Just Raven.

Later that night, promptly at six o'clock, Taylor and her parents arrived. She looks as disgusted to see Raven as she was to see her.

"Hello, this is for you," Taylor's mom handed Blair a bowl of salad and bread.

"You shouldn't have!" Blair gave a high-pitched squeal. Her work voice was in full effect.

Raven stood by herself while The French Family took off their coats, and Blair collected them. *This was really happening,* Raven thought, *and I can't do a thing about it.*

Raven glanced down at her phone in her hand. Six-o-seven. It was going to be a long night.

CHAPTER 11

The group sat around the kitchen table making small talk. Well, at least the parents were. Raven's dad wasn't home from work yet, and Blair and the Frenchs seemed to be long-lost friends. Raven was relieved when she heard the familiar jingle of her father's car keys opening the front door. He always lightened the mood, and Raven couldn't think of anything more needed right now.

"We got dinner with Obama's, he strolled into the kitchen in his Lake Lacroix uniform and a sheepish smile. Raven laughed but felt like she shouldn't have. Taylor didn't laugh. Raven could tell by her dad's stroll that he was embarrassed for being late. Raven just knew her dad that way. The jingle of his keys. The pep in his step. He went to Blair and kissed her forehead.

"Hello, Mr. Jamison," Mrs. French stood.

"I'm Ebony French, this is my husband — Darryl."

Mr. French rose from his seat and greeted Khalil with a handshake.

"Hey, my man," Khalil said. The men dabbed each other, and Mr. French straightened his tie.

"Your plate is over there, honey," Blair pointed Khalil to the kitchen. She was lighting candles around the dining room and drawing the blinds. Blair couldn't see it, but Raven could make out the Marshall's price tag still stuck to the side of the candle from her seat. Blair had run out that morning and bought new candles to replace the ones Carter had hacked into the week before.

"Thanks, honey, let me run upstairs and change," Khalil nodded.

The waiting. The downtime when their parents were talking *at* them and *about* them but not including them in the conversation. There was a clinking of a glass. The match sound of the lighter. Blair rummaging in the kitchen or Mrs. French looking around the room, noticing all the family pictures. It was during those quick moments with nothingness that Raven and Taylor silently quarreled, reading each other from the sides of their eyes. This was the hardest part for Raven. When there was nothing left to say so they had to make eye contact.

As Raven trained her eyes to settle on everything in the room except Taylor French — Khalil walked in now wearing ball shorts and a t-shirt. He didn't even try to dress up as Raven eyed him up and down. The only thing he was missing was his man flops. She saw her mom eyeing his attire. Khalil finally sat down and joined everyone else at the table. "So Raven, I hear you two go to school together," Khalil cut into his steak and motioned to Raven and Taylor with his fork.

It had begun.

"Yes, Dad," I said, with as much nothingness as I could muster.

"Yes, Mr. Jamison, we are also on the dance team together," Taylor said in a soft voice.

Raven couldn't read Taylor's emotions. She was cagey like a cat. Taylor's voice didn't sound like nothingness. But it didn't sound like something either. At least not yet.

"Taylor, I didn't realize you guys danced together?" Mrs. French sat up in her chair.

"For the past two years, Mom. I told you that," Taylor said. Mrs. French turned towards Taylor and looked at her a second longer.

The extra second made it seem prolonged.

Awkward.

More nothingness.

Taylor knew that look in Mrs. French's eyes. Blair had just given that same look to Raven a few hours earlier when they discussed Taylor coming over.

Shade. Raven detected the shade.

"She's the captain," Khalil said proudly to everyone and no one.

"Oh?" Mrs. French declared, turning away from Taylor. Taylor shrank in her seat a little.

"Yea, she is Mom," Taylor blurted.

"How does that work, do you guys come up with the dances as a team, or do you get to choose Raven?"

Raven paused before responding. Another second too long. "I like for us all to choose the dances. If there's something we all agree on, then we'll dance to that. We haven't really disagreed too many times about dance routines, though."

Blair nodded her head in approval. Raven felt like she had just given her best performance, and her mom was proud. Taylor was acting for Mrs. French the same way Raven was for her Mom.

"And Taylor? Have you ever wanted to be captain?" Mrs. French asked, turning towards Taylor. The way she asked. . . it-it, sounded more like an accusation than a question.

"Yes, I've thought about it," Taylor mumbled. This time Raven could read her.

Honesty.

"Dang it," Khalil interrupted. "Guess we won't have time to Huddle tonight." He snapped his fingers and gave a smirk.

Raven giggled to herself.

Khalil liked Huddle the least because he had to talk about himself. But, here he was sacrificing himself for the sake of the conversation for Mom's job. I guess he was tap dancing too: everyone was on their best behavior tonight.

"What's Huddle?" Taylor asked.

Raven explained to Taylor what their nightly ritual of Huddle consisted of, and she could see Taylor's parents looking at each other.

"We all just squat somewhere in front of the TV. I can't remember the last time we ate together," Mrs. French chuckled.

Mr. French and Taylor didn't laugh.

"Everyone eats in their own rooms," Taylor added.

Mr. and Mrs. French looked at each other again.

"So, you do this every night?" Taylor quizzed.

"Yea, most nights." Raven's voice was low.

"But not tonight!" Khalil boasted, woofing potatoes into his mouth and breaking the silence that was forming around the dinner table.

He had no couth, Raven thought. But tonight, it was okay with her. Blair could be mad at both together.

They finished the dinner, and it wasn't as painful as Raven had expected.

She and Taylor exchanged a few glances, but it seemed like Taylor was trying to avoid Raven just as much. This concerned her. Why would Taylor not want to deal with her? Raven was clear about why she didn't like Taylor, but she was unsure about Taylor's reasonings.

Raven later stood in the kitchen in her pajamas and slippers, loading the dishwasher. She mulled over the circumstances of the night and just couldn't place Taylor's mood, and that bothered her. She had been steamrolled tonight. The culprit? Her mom. Blair seemed pleased with the result, and she immediately called her supervisor excited because she landed the French account.

Raven had watched Taylor throughout the night. Her head held high. Hair perfectly coiffed and clothes always in place. If Raven didn't have her *Brown Girls Club*, Raven would probably be jealous of Taylor. *But that made little sense either*, Raven contended. Why would she need other people to help her feel less jealous of someone else? Raven stood there, swirling dishes in the sink as she rinsed them with water, letting her thoughts get the best of her. Were her reasons for not liking Taylor even warranted? Raven couldn't remember the last time they had an actual conversation. Raven just knew Taylor seemed to throw her shade whenever they were in dance class or school. Raven finished loading the dishwasher and put the food away. She wiped down the counters and shut the lights off behind her before heading upstairs for bed. She just couldn't shake Taylor.

Taylor seemed so . . . amicable during dinner. It was probably an act for her parents.

Raven whipped out her cell phone and called Trinity; she answered on the first ring.

"Finally, girl, I was waiting for forever! Jasmine texted me and said, what was going down! I had my brother call my phone just to make sure it was working."

Raven giggled. Trinity was so extra.

Raven shared the night's events with Trinity and Mrs. French's questions about the dance team.

"I wonder what that's about," Trinity mulled.

Raven wondered the same thing.

"So, she was nice-nasty, huh?" Trinity said, recapping for herself.

"Nice-nasty?"

"Yea, she wasn't entirely nice, but she also wasn't nasty. She was *nice- nasty*."

"Where do you get this stuff from?" Raven chuckled as she laid across her bed.

"I don't know, Ray. I don't know about this one. I'm not even sure what really started all of this."

"Something is telling me maybe I need to look at this a little differently," Raven said. She twirled one of her curls with her free hand. "She really did nothing to me. We've just never liked each other."

"But Raven, I still wouldn't trust her," Trinity's voice sounded full of concern. "Don't forget, you may not have had issues with Taylor, but you had a little altercation with Jessica."

"Altercation is a strong word."

Raven thought about Jessica. They had stood toe to toe eighth grade in the nurse's office, ready to rumble. Jessica thought it was amusing to tell everyone Raven had on fake Nikes that day — which Raven didn't — and tried to get everyone to make fun of her. Raven made the mistake of thinking they were friends, and she invited Jessica over to her house. Raven's mom had just bought her fresh pair of sneakers, and after Jessica left Raven's house that day, Raven never saw those shoes again. She looked high and low and even checked the lost and found at school. But inside, she seethed. Raven knew the shoes hadn't been lost, but they had been found — by Jessica. Not long after the missing shoes came the rumor about fake Nikes. Raven told Jessica that day, *"Don't worry about these shoes, worry about these hands."* That was one of the first times Raven remembered sticking up for herself. Truth be told, Raven had never been in a fight before.

But she still wasn't no punk.

The school had called both of their parents. Jessica's mom picked her up and reamed her out all the way to the car. Blair picked Raven up and took her for ice cream to celebrate. Raven hadn't had a problem with Jessica since. When Taylor moved to Lake Lacroix from NOLA in the middle of eighth grade, it seemed to Raven they joined forces and set their sights on Raven.

"Just be mindful of everything, I guess. I'm just saying don't fix things with Taylor and then have to fight the last level of loco with Jessica. Don't forget they are a package deal."

She was right. They were a packaged deal just like Raven was with her girls, and there was no breaking that up.

Trinity was right. She would play her position and just wait.

CHAPTER 12

Raven rushed from her last class of the day, her book bag flapping behind her back. Raven knew she shouldn't have stayed after-school to talk to Amir. Here she was, racing through the hallways — late for dance.

Amir wanted to talk about their chemistry project coming up after Halloween. They had partnered up; Amir was good at numbers, and Raven was good at putting it all together. They had different opinions about what their project should be. He wanted something to do with basketball. What in the world was a basketball chemistry project? Raven wanted to make crystals. It was super easy, and Raven knew how to do it. They settled somewhere in the middle and decided they would be lowering the temperature of water and ice to make sugar crystals.

Amir had spent the weekend in NOLA with his family. His skin was darker, he had gotten a tan, and Raven could detect tiny freckles poking through his skin. When he turned his face towards the sky, the sun danced across his face illuminating his Melanin. He was still beautiful; Raven would give him that.

She was slightly jealous of Amir's time with his family. He was having all types of fun, and she was envious listening to him talk about their fish fry and BBQ. A seemingly normal and calm weekend compared to what hers had become. Raven and Amir were only supposed to meet for about twenty minutes, but time escaped Raven when she and Amir were together. *Go to dance practice today or meet with Amir?* As Raven raced down the hallway, she had already made her choice.

Raven dashed down the long corridor hallway to the gym and did her best to hold on to the books in her hand, but she ended up dropping them anyway. Her books hit the floor with a loud slap, and students peeked out of their after-school classes to see what all the commotion was about.

"S-s-sorry," Raven rushed, stuffing her papers back into her binder.

She was all discombobulated today. She quickly picked her things off the floor and raced into the gym. Raven burst through the door, and the entire team was dropped to the mat doing squats and leg presses. They looked at Raven as she ran up to them out of breath.

Taylor stood and tapped her foot, looking at the clock. Nia stood next to Taylor, scowling at her.

"Our leader is here, ladies." Taylor ridiculed; her arms now folded. Raven tried to ignore her.

"Give me a second, I have to change my clothes."

"She has to change her clothes, ladies," Taylor repeated and turned around on her heel.

Raven heard one of her goons somewhere suck their teeth. . . she would deal with them later. She hurriedly changed into her dance uniform and rushed back into the gym. Nia turned on the warmup music and looked at Raven. Nia's eyes were concerned. Raven's eyes were pleading. *You really should have prepared for today a little bit better,* Raven fussed at herself. Ms. Adams, their dance coach, already said she was going to miss practice that day, and Raven was in charge. Raven picked that day of all days to be late.

And Taylor chose that day to be an asshole.

One of them would have an issue.

The team warmed up for fifteen minutes, and Taylor, who was usually in the rear because she was one of their tallest dancers, shimmied and moved her way to the front of the squad. She was now dancing next to Raven. Nia was also usually in the back, and she danced her way up too. Taylor stood on Raven's left and Nia to the right. Raven stood in the center. Nia always had Raven's back, and her right. Raven struggled to remember the steps feverishly practiced weeks before. She had chosen those steps, with help from the team, of course. Now she couldn't seem to remember any of them. Today had been a rough day, and Raven had been counting and breathing all day long, practicing calming herself. Raven had even stopped by Ms. Whitaker's office on a whim, but she wasn't in today.

She was on her own again, it seemed.

Raven struggled to keep her mind focused. She looked up at the lights in the gym, and they blinded her eyes, now pooling with tears.

"You good?" Nia mouthed.

Raven nodded her head. She would have to be.

She recounted the day in her head. Khalil had to take her to school in the cop car when she woke up late. Usually, Raven enjoyed riding with him, but the silence between them was deafening. Raven lost in her own thoughts and Khalil in his.

Blair also woke up on the wrong side of the bed. The art gallery lost a big sponsor who went with another agency. She was thinking about going back to work — full-time.

And Carter.

Well, Carter was Carter. They now had to watch for critters in his room. There was so much food stashed everywhere that Blair had to go in again and clean it out. Carter was at school when Blair cleaned the room, and when he returned, he packed his bags and called Ms. Cottman again. We didn't even know Carter reached out to Ms. Cottman this time until she showed up that night during dinner and said Carter said he couldn't live here anymore. After a tense family meeting, he stayed. Blair agreed not to clean his room without his consent. Everyone seemed in survival mode and handled things differently. They were bursting at the seams.

Raven snapped back to the routine as she accidentally tripped over her own feet.

Crap! Raven thought.

She glanced at Taylor, now studying her intently with a raised eyebrow.

Raven wished to be anywhere but there. She needed to cry and could feel it deep down in her chest, a deep soul cry began to rise, it needed to be unleashed.

But not here, not now — and not in front of Taylor.

Raven made it through practice with Taylor and Nia by her side, each for different reasons.

“Okay, thanks, guys, that’s it for today. Again, sorry for being late,” Raven said to the girls as they wiped sweat. They grabbed their bags and headed for the locker rooms.

Taylor grabbed her bag as well and turned to walk out of the gym.

“Can I talk to you for a second?” Raven was curt.

Taylor froze. So did Nia. She dropped her bag and walked towards Raven.

“Do we have a problem?” Raven turned too and met Taylor halfway. Taylor took a step back as Nia inched closer.

"Do we?" Taylor challenged.

"You've had issues with me for years, and I'm not sure why. So, I'm asking."

"Maybe the problem is you," Taylor pointed her finger in Raven's face.

"You're always rolling your eyes and smirking at me. I say nothing to you. So, if you have a problem, we can deal with it. I'm tired." Raven's voice trembled, and her hands shook. She stood taller, though, having shared her truth. "So, do you want to fight?" Nia took off her gym bag. Nia was always ready and didn't mince words.

"No . . . we don't have a problem," Taylor said, with wider eyes. "You made that post last year on Instagram. About my family. " Huh?" Raven was so confused.

"What post, what are you talking about? "

"You made a post about my dad. Him moving out."

"Again, I don't know what you're talking about." Raven was still confused.

Taylor fumbled through her bag and retrieved her cell phone. She scrolled for a minute. Raven could see the reflection of Instagram shining through Taylor's eyes. She was searching through posts.

"This one," she turned her phone towards Raven. Raven studied the post from Raven's page. It was a meme featuring an interracial couple; it read: *Stop arguing with Darryl. Darryl will ruin your credit. Jake will take you on vacation.* Raven paused. Taylor lived with her parents in East Lake Lacroix, where all the big houses sat. She went over to Taylor's house a few times before she decided she didn't like Taylor. Her family even had a maid! Taylor's dad's name was Darryl. The woman in the meme left her boyfriend for a White man named Jake. She thought the post was about her dad, Darryl. *But why would Taylor's parents pretend to be together at dinner last month?* Raven's mind moved, putting all the pieces together. Maybe the French family was playing a role, just like the Jamison family.

"Taylor," Raven breathed. "This was not about your dad. I just thought it was funny."

Unphased by Raven's words, Taylor stood stern.

"So, you didn't know my Dad moved out?"

"No. How would I know that? Your parents were just at my house?" Raven reflected.

"Well, you and Jasmine were laughing when I walked by your class that day. As soon as you saw me, you laughed."

"When?"

"Couple weeks ago," Taylor sighed.

"I knew nothing about your dad or your family. And I don't remember laughing with Jasmine. I'm sorry you think I said something about you, but I didn't."

Taylor's chest heaved, and she sobbed loudly as much as she tried not to. The floodgates had opened.

Nia stood watch, letting Raven and Taylor talk.

"Raven, I don't believe you," Taylor's voice was sharp and pained now. "You knew, and you always knew. You think because you have both your parents, and you're team captain?, and don't talk about my family when your family and your aunt —"

"Taylor," Raven interrupted.

"I'm sorry. I really am. But I'm not your enemy. None of that was intentional, but I'm sorry you feel that way." She was earnest in her apology.

"You know people told me about you. They said you play the victim. They say you hide behind your friends. They already knew it. But I still tried with you. I'm done trying —"

"Taylor, what are you talking about?" Raven questioned. *Playing the victim? Wow. That was a new one,* Raven thought..

"I play the victim? No, I don't! I think you believe that!" Raven's voice was raised now too, and she was ready to spew venom.

Taylor had called her out, said that she played the victim. Taylor didn't know how hard Raven tried to stay to herself. Raven playing the victim couldn't be further from the truth.

"You know what, I'm outta here," Taylor grabbed her bags and stomped toward the door.

"Taylor!" Raven screamed. Raven wanted to finish the conversation once and for all and hear what Taylor had to say. They were on two totally different chapters in two different books. Taylor stormed out of the gym and slammed the door against the wall on her way out.

Raven stopped chasing behind her.

CHAPTER 13

Raven sat in the bathtub, sweat running down the sides of her face. Her knees were pulled up to her chest, and she had lit a candle. Candles usually calmed her down, but today it reminded her how she felt.

On fire. Out of control.

Taylor cried. Raven remembered the look in her eyes. Pained. Afraid.

Raven had never known herself to make someone else feel like that. She thought about their friendship or lack thereof. She and Taylor were never friends, but somehow, they still didn't like each other. Raven struggled to remember the IG post Taylor showed her. It seemed to be a catalyst for so much of this, but at the same time, for none of it at all.

The meme was so funny to Raven when she posted it — she had even taken a screenshot and sent it to Nia. She had no idea Taylor took offense to it, or even how she saw it; Raven's IG page was private. She thought Raven had talked about her family. Raven remembered the awkward dinner they had a few weeks ago. The hard look Mrs. French had given to Taylor.

Raven's assumptions from that night were correct, the French's had been actors, and Taylor had the lead role — mediating between the two families.

Raven thought about Ms. Whitaker. *"Perception is everything,"* she always said. She was damned if Ms. Whitaker wasn't right again. Raven ran her loofah up and down her bare arm staring at her brown flesh and reflected.

Somehow, they were sparring over things that could have been squashed. Raven's dad was adamant about being mindful of social media posts. He saw so many teenagers at the station caught up in internet situations when they were Catfished or Swatted. Raven always laughed at him when he told her these things.

How could those kids be so stupid? She wondered. That would never be Raven, she was smarter than that. She'd never argue online about a boy — that was the ultimate betrayal, and she shuddered at the thought. But somehow, she had gotten caught up anyway. This time without her knowledge. And Nana — because all Nana talked about was supporting other Black women. Less fighting, more *'sista-girl-fran'* going on. Had she supported Taylor or shamed her?

Am I going too hard on myself? Raven dwelled.

Everything was so confusing right now.

Maybe she was the toxic one? Raven was so concerned about how everyone else treated her she failed to even consider the possibility that she might be the common denominator here. Goosebumps formed on Raven's arms even though it wasn't cold. The thought made her headache. She placed so much emphasis on her friends, but was she a mean girl and didn't know it? Had she become the silent bully to others? Taylor said that she hid behind her friends. That statement angered her — but was there truth to it? Raven did so much to fly under the radar, with her friends and out of the way.

Raven wasn't so sure anymore.

Blair and Raven spent many days talking about friendship. Blair shared with Raven the importance of surrounding yourself with good people. Friends who would confront you about yourself. Had Raven's friends confronted her or been aware of Raven's semi toxic behavior with Taylor? And did they address Raven about it? Had she been receptive?

It was just so much to think about.

Raven shuddered as she turned the scalding water back on. The steam burned her skin, but she didn't shut it off. Blair's words echoed in Raven's mind once again:

"Always support your circle like they support you. Make sure when you all huddle up, you're not bumping heads. Make sure when you're rowing, they're not drilling holes in the back."

"I know, Mom." Raven had sighed.

But did she know? She scrubbed her skin with the loofah harder. What kind of friend was she? What kind of cousin? And daughter? Raven questioned her role in everyone's life. Was she the weakest link?

She dunked her head under the water and held her breath for a second. Then a second longer. Then a second longer. Raven felt the water swallow her hair, soaking like a sponge. Her lungs burned as she held her breath. She held it there for a few seconds, wanting to disappear.

Just a second... . Another second. . . Another second... . Raven's chest was on fire and felt heavy. She stayed under water a little while longer. Moments later, Raven opened her eyes and was jolted out of the bathtub by Carter's arms. He had pulled her up by the shoulders, his eyes wide with fear and concern. Carter held onto Raven as if he had brought her back to life. He banged on her back, and Raven coughed up water and spit as she struggled to capture her breath. Snot ran down her nose; she was dry heaving and gasping for air. Raven's lungs were searing now. They were ablaze like the candle next to her she stared into earlier.

She stood there naked and sneezing, with red bloodshot eyes. As she struggled to catch her breath, Carter threw her a towel and ran out of the bathroom.

Raven felt rage build up inside of her, and she angrily wrapped her towel around her body and marched out of the bathroom. Her wet feet slapped against the hardwood floors, and her squishy toes slipped beneath her. She approached Carter's room and raised her arm to bang on the door, but something stopped her, and she hesitated.

She put her hand down and lightly touched Carter's door; too light for him to hear. She worked to calm herself. She panted, and water pooled around her, it dripped from her face and hair down to her feet on the floor. Raven replaced her arm back by her side. She turned and walked back into her room and softly shut her door. She plopped on her bed with the towel tight around her chest. Her hair dripped, and her chest still felt on fire. She grabbed her cell phone and, with wet hands, texted Amir, asking if he was up. Raven wasn't sure what she tried to do in the tub. She just wanted the thoughts to stop and for things to be quiet — if only for a second. Raven's face was flushed with embarrassment. Her stomach churned, threatening to erupt. Chills set in, and her body shuddered. Her phone buzzed, and it was Amir calling on Facetime. His face flashed across the screen, and Raven's eyes misted. She didn't say a word while Amir's even voice soothed, "You're okay. You're okay..."

After she told him what happened, Amir joked and repeated the phrase, "You're okay. We'll stick to showers from now on." A chortle escaped Raven's mouth, and she collapsed onto her bed, her curls fell around her face. She fell asleep to Amir's face — phone in hand.

The next morning, Raven heard her bathroom door open while in the shower. She was in a better mood, but she could tell by her mom's tone that was about to change.

"Rayyy, I need a favor. Can you take Carter with you to class?" Blair shouted over the running water. It was a cool Saturday morning, and Raven was dressing for Nana's Yoga class down at the Y.

"Maaa, I can't, I'm meeting the girls there."

"Your dad is at the station, and I have to run into the gallery to meet a buyer."

"Aren't you still on leave?"

"Yes, but I've been working on this sale for a while, and we need the money."

"Needed the money," she said. Raven speculated; Carter was eating them out of a house and home, consuming so much food from the table and the other stuff hidden in his room. Of course, they needed the money — they needed to buy food.

Blair stood in the bathroom doorway, waiting for Raven's response. Raven shut off the water and grabbed her towel from the rack.

"Okay, Mom," she conceded.

“Thanks so much, Ray, I'll drop you guys off, so try to be ready in twenty minutes,” She blew kisses and closed the bathroom door.

Raven sighed and wrapped the towel tighter around her body. She searched her room for something comfortable to wear. She spent the first five minutes of every morning doing squats to plump up her butt, but she would have to skip this morning. She needed to ensure Carter was dressed in what she deemed appropriate for a day out with her and her friends. Who knows what he was thinking these days?

Raven found some tights and a long sleeve “Do the Right Thing” t-shirt. She grabbed her BGC jacket and checked herself over in the mirror. Satisfied, she opened her bedroom door and stomped down the hall to Carter's room. Carter swung his own door open as Raven was about to enter, and they almost collided in the hallway.

“Oh, you are ready!” Raven exclaimed, giving him a once over. Carter was wearing a plain navy-blue sweatsuit and sneakers. *Acceptable,* she mulled. “Let's go,” she said. Carter followed.

Blair waited in the driveway with the car running while Raven and Carter hopped in. Raven looked at Carter in the backseat. These days, he reminded her of the girl from *The Exorcist*. He was fine one minute and psycho the next. He scratched his head and looked out the window. They didn't talk about the bathtub incident the night before. She wasn't sure why he barged into the bathroom last night, but she saw fear in his eyes for the second time. Now in the car, she noticed a dent on the side of his head — just like her dad. She hadn't seen that before.

Still, he looks fine to me. Like a normal kid, Raven brooded. But something in his eyes told her that he wasn't. She wished she could somehow get through to her younger cousin. Before the bathtub fiasco, they met Carter's newest therapist, Ms. Margaret. Blair already fired one who fell asleep on the job. Literally fell asleep on the job. It was her second session with Carter, and she showed him a video. Blair and Raven came back from food shopping and walked in on Carter and his therapist. Khalil was in the garage working on his car — supervising, but not supervising. They entered the living room where Carter sat, and sure enough, the therapist was snoring away, sitting in an almost upright position in the corner chair — asleep. Carter was watching *Wildin Out* on TV and eating Oreos. That was the end of her. Blair went on and on about it, and naturally, Khalil had endless sleepwalking jokes.

Ms. Margaret looked about Ms. Whitaker's age. She seemed nice. Raven hoped she got through to Carter. *"Healing needs to be a family affair. It would be more beneficial to him if his family members were engaged as well,"* Ms. Margaret had said. Without question, they all agreed. Raven understood it too. In school, she hated individual sessions with Ms. Whitaker but didn't mind group sessions. This was like a group session for Carter. Blair was always about that life for Carter, and she would make sure everyone else was too.

Khalil was harder to convince.

CHAPTER 14

Carter

Aunt B pulled up to Lake Lacroix Y. The building was old and desperately needed updating. Carter remembered taking swim lessons there just a few years ago. His mom was serious about swimming lessons; Carter would know how to swim. His mom told him that she lost an old friend who drowned at Lake Lanier in Georgia. *"No one should ever have to go through something like that. All White people know how to swim, but not us."* She pointed to her hand and motioned to her skin. *Not us.* Carter wondered if Raven knew how to swim and if she received the same scared straight story.

Nia tapped on the door and jarred Carter out of his thoughts. Raven hopped out the other side, and Aunt B blew kisses and pulled off as soon as he shut the door.

"She didn't even say bye," Raven noted.

Aunt B beeped to Nana, who held the door open for Carter and the girls. Raven walked over to Jasmine, Nia, and Trinity while Carter stood by himself off to the side. Raven and her friends looked cold, and their noses were pink.

They were fresh-faced and ready for their morning session. Meanwhile, Carter scowled at being woken up so early.

"Ms. Phoenix, your skin looks amazing!" Trinity shouted.

"I know, right? I keep telling ya'll Black girls need sunscreen too. That's all this is here, water and sunscreen. Y'all know that Black don't crack." Nana flashed a grin.

"Well, what sunscreen do you use?" Trinity leaned in and was so serious. "Didn't you just hear me, girl? It's called *'Black Girl Sunscreen'* you'll never forget it." She and Trinity shared a laugh.

"Hey, Brown Girl!" Jasmine moved a curl out of Raven's face.

"Hey, Girl!" Raven beamed.

Carter stood with his hands in his pockets and hoodie up when Trinity walked over and greeted him. Carter nodded his head at Trinity and turned away, annoyed. Why did she say hi to him in front of everyone? Of course, they all turned to look. He hoped she didn't expect more conversation because he was not in the mood.

"All right y'all, come inside and sit down, sit down, let's get started." Nana rushed everyone in, checking her Apple watch.

The inside of Nana's yoga studio stood in stark contrast to the outside of the YMCA. The hardwood floors were quiet. Nana required socks or bare feet in the space. *"Better for grounding,"* she said. If you stood just right while barefoot on the hardwood, the floor had some spring to it and would bounce you up — just a little. Red brick was exposed on the walls and in the corners of the room sat ceiling lights pointing down. The lights were dim, never shining too much on anyone or anything. Carter heard the faint sound of drums and humming. He smelled a musky, woodsy scent making its way through the room, and a soft haze was floating in the air. Nana put a lot of care and attention into the space. She wanted the energy to be just right and for everyone to come into the space, taking what they needed and leaving what they didn't. Carter observed everything around him as he stood against the wall. Nana's studio was growing by leaps and bounds and created a different vibe to the building from when he took swim lessons. Her classes may have been the reason the YMCA was still around — Nana had brought the crowds! Carter liked the space. It smelled good, not like that fruity stuff Aunt B preferred.

In the front of the room sat Nana. Everyone followed her lead and knelt onto their mats. Her hands rested on her chest, and she began inhaling and exhaling. She took longer and more pronounced breaths. Nana bent forward and rang a bell she had in a small, gold bowl. Carter felt drumming from the bowl in his chest. The infectious sound moved throughout the room as Nana rang the bowl in circular motions one last time before sitting them down. She crouched over and leaned forward, placing her hands together in worship. Without words, the group followed suit, mirroring Nana's movements. Carter peered at Raven from the corner of his eye as she struggled to loosen her legs. Carter was going to enjoy Nana's yoga class because the expectation was stillness. Quietness.

Raven caught Carter's eye, and he shut his — blocking her out. She was always looking at him, and she never said anything about saving her last night. He knew what she was up to; he saw it too many times with his mom.

"Okay, team, let's transition into Warrior 2 pose," Nana rose to her feet. "Plant yourself. Rest yourself. Imagine grounding your body to Mother Earth." Carter peeked a little through shut eyes, and Nana now wore a headset. He could hear her voice through the speakers. Carter stole one more glance in Raven's direction. She hadn't transitioned into the pose yet. "Extend your arms from both ends. Pull those fingertips. Make sure your knees are straight and tucked behind your feet. We are perched. Ready for battle. We are ready for whatever. We are *No Limit Soldiers*, Nana soothed.

Raven snorted, and Carter peeked at her again.

Nana purred, "Feel the energy coursing through you. Feel your bloodline, the strength you come from. You're doubting yourself — Don't. Don't worry about not getting through it. Pray about what it's going to look like on the other side after you get over it."

Carter wondered if Nana was talking to him. She had to be. Carter's arm twitched. He stole another peek in Raven's direction; this time, her pose was strong. Intense. Her chest was poked out.

Carter shut his eyes again.

Walking around the room, Nana touched their shoulders. Carter could smell Nana's lavender shea butter. "Your presence is needed and wanted. Don't hide yourself from anyone. You stand tall like the mighty oaks outside. Storm after storm. Trial after trial, they stay in place. They are the same," she said, pausing in front of Raven.

Nana stood in front of Carter next and lifted his arm higher, correcting his posture. "They are the same," Nana repeated. "Even when they feel weak like they can't hold on anymore, they still stand. Rooted in themselves. Whole. Full and unashamed." She moved to Trinity.

The group transitioned next into *Savasana* pose as Nana instructed. Carter lay down on his back, his shoulders and neck loose. He didn't remember which school it was he attended, but he did this before during gym class. Anything that didn't require him to talk he liked. Nana's voice was now almost above a whisper. The music changed, and he heard water dropping after a rainstorm. The boom of the water sound resonated in his chest again. He felt it in his stomach as he lay flat on the mat. His arm still twitched, but by breathing, Carter was getting better at controlling it.

"We quieted our mind and our souls. Let's relax our bodies. They do so much for us. Let's recharge our hearts." Nana walked throughout the room ... "Forgive yourself, love yourself. Be kind to your bodies and each other."

The floor cracked beneath her bare feet.

"Take three deep breaths, and inhale, and inhale, and inhale. . . and exhale as deep as you can. Again. Inhale and inhale. Imagine a bright, white light coursing through your body. It's healing to you. Exhale the stress, the anger. The things that keep our body in survival mode. Let's exhale those things. We are loved, we are honored, we are celebrated. . . Just breathe," Nana instructed.

Listening to Nana's voice, Carter tried to clear his mind. His stomach seemed to be permanently in knots these days. So many grownups made choices for him. Hearing Nana speak, his stomach didn't feel so tight, and he exhaled.

"Now count to three," Nana whispered. "One, two, three. One, two, three." The room was quiet. Calm. Carter peeked again and saw Nana standing next to Raven.

"The light in me honors the light in you," Nana said.

"The light in me honors the light in you," everyone repeated back.

Nana bent down next to Carter and said it again in a hushed voice only the two of them could hear. No one else heard the words in the dimly lit room.

"The light in me honors the light in you," Nana breathed.

With a cracked voice, he returned the words, *"The light in me honors the light in you."*

Carter finally spoke.

CHAPTER 15
Blair

Across town, Blair drove through the streets with the windows down. Jhene Aiko was on the radio singing about a time when she was young and wanted to have fun. The song should have gone with a fun and lighthearted Blair. Not Blair today.

She had lied.

She told her family she needed to go to the gallery, but truth be told — she needed a moment to herself. Blair pulled into the park and ride area at Lake Lacroix. It was incredibly beautiful; she understood why Raven spent so much time here. The water glistened and made waves as the fisherman worked. The sun warmed Blair's skin, and there was a slight chill; she tightened her sweater around her waist. Blair could feel the cool breeze through her locs with the windows cracked. It was never cold in Lake Lacroix, but along with the ice that crept into Blair's spirit, it could have been a blizzard in November.

Carefully, she backed into a far corner off to the left, the closest to the water and furthest away from everyone. She threw the car in park and rummaged around in her purse until she found it. Next, she searched through her glove box, tossing stacks of napkins until she found her lighter. Blair lit up the tiny piece, closed her eyes, and inhaled. She took one puff... . then one more — this time inhaling deeper. She exhaled, and sour smoke filled the car. Blair didn't smoke often, sometimes it made her restless. But this time, she needed it to calm her mind, even if for just a moment. Blair exhaled and wondered how the kids made out. Time spent together was rare these days. Everyone rushed off in different directions and found reasons to be apart. Carter still wasn't speaking. Blair made a mental note to text Ms. Margaret again. And Raven. *How could I have ever forgotten about Taylor?* Raven told her about it so many times. She and Raven had always been close, and Blair valued their relationship. So many of Blair's colleagues complained about their children, expecting perfection from them. Nitpicking at so many things. Blair felt lucky that Raven still considered her an ally against high school and teenage life. Raven was a worrywart, and that worried Blair. Maybe that made Blair a worrywart too, and that's where Raven got her issues from. They brought it out of each other because they got it from each other. Mother and daughter.

Blair spoke to Ms. Whitaker the week prior for an update on Raven's in-school sessions. Ms. Whitaker discussed Raven's growth from last year until now. She mentioned Raven's struggle with Carter's move in. She ended the conversation casually mentioning Raven was friendly with a boy named Amir.

"Excuse me?" Blair whispered and gripped the phone tighter. She wasn't sure she had heard her correctly.

"*Raven is friendly with a boy,"* Ms. Whitaker repeated. She explained that Raven often discussed Amir in their sessions.

Blair felt slightly jealous. Just slightly. Raven was trusting Ms. Whitaker with information she hadn't even mentioned to her yet. And when had that changed? She and Raven discussed things together, and now Raven was doing her own thing and going at it alone. But that thought saddened Blair too. Isn't that what you want your child to do? Be independent and, when necessary, go at it alone in the world?

Blair puffed again and sank lower in her seat. There had been so many other things on her mind that she couldn't keep everything straight. Some things suffered; something or someone always suffered when the family feuded.

Blair snorted as smoke caught in her throat. She coughed and blinked back tears. Her throat burned.

Blair carefully inhaled this time....

There was something about going home to a beautiful Black man every day that still excited her. As her relationship with Khalil grew, their priorities changed, and their focus shifted towards the future and creating their legacy. Raven often asked about her grandparents, but Blair rarely talked about them. There wasn't much to say in her eyes. She didn't have a typical childhood, but it wasn't a bad one by any stretch of the imagination. She would show Raven pictures. There was an endless array of Grand Canyon, Empire State Building, and other places the family visited. This was all she would give Raven, coupled with a few tidbits of wisdom.

"The family you create is more important than the family you come from," she told Raven. That was her way of ending the conversation when Raven asked. Raven probably had so many questions that she shushed along. The memories, although not as colorful as some people's, made Blair sad. Her heart sank. She had tried to empower Raven to be the best brown girl she could be, but Blair cut off large parts of her own history by trying to move forward and create something new. Blair Trinidad was an only child. She didn't have any siblings or cousins. It was just the three of them. It was always that way.

Blair's parents had been older and more mature than her friends' parents. Both were intellectuals; they went to museums and read books. Long weekends were spent at medical conferences for Dr. Trinidad, *the Black Veterinarian.* Sometimes he even referred to himself that way. Blair didn't know if it was a way of stating the obvious before White people exclaimed, "Oh, you're a veterinarian!" Or — if he wore it as a badge of honor.

Sometimes both. Mrs. Trinidad complained that Mr. Trinidad *tap-danced* a little too much. Blair's mom was a schoolteacher. When the Trinidad's neighbors gathered around the TV for Sunday Night Football and family fun, Blair took Spanish lessons. A future *"necessary life skill,"* they promised.

When Blair was twenty years old, she sat in her dorm room at Xavier University when her phone rang. It was her dad's lawyer. Both of her parents had passed away in a car crash coming back from the American Veterinary Medical Association Conference. Blair remembered it so clearly . . . She spoke to them right before they got on the road. They were excited because normally, none of the conferences were in driving distance — but this conference was the exception. *"Stretch out on the highway,"* Mr. Trinidad had smiled. A drunk driver had hit her parents, and there had been no survivors.

Her world instantly changed.

Burying a parent at a young age changes you. Does something to you as a person. You go from the world being at your fingertips and your age being your advantage to now being your disadvantage. Your hindrance. To the world, it's the *thing* that holds you back. With age comes experience, and people take you seriously. Every time you see someone older, they want to know your family's name.

"Who ya peoples is? Who's ya, Mama?" they ask. It was a constant reminder of what was lost and what still was unknown about life, an empty feeling having no one connected to you. Not anymore.

Who do you go to for answers? Who do you talk to when you don't understand deductibles? What was a deductible anyway? She was now forty-four years old, and she still didn't quite get it. Where did you go when you wanted to make sure the mechanic wasn't taking advantage of you because you were a woman? Who would sit proud as you graduated—whispering, *that's my baby, that's my baby. . .* Life. . . Blair knew nothing about life when she became an orphan, her parents navigated these things for her. For months she lived life in a stupor, struggling to cope.

One particularly bad semester when Blair almost flunked out, she took an African American studies course. Blair was versed on her lineage and where she came from. Mr. and Mrs. Trinidad understood regardless of their social status and Blair's lighter skin, she was still a Black woman in America. As Malcolm X put it best, she was: "The most disrespected, unprotected, and neglected person in America." And for that reason, Mr. and Mrs. Trinidad made sure to tell her she descended from royalty. The world just hadn't caught on yet.

During this course in college, Blair heard the stories of her ancestors differently than she ever had before. She read and read whatever she could get her hands on relating to her people. She felt a deep, visceral reaction to the plight of her ancestry. Blair learned about Queen Nandi, Henrietta Lacks, Claudette Colvin, Shirley Chisholm, Arthur Ashe, Recy Taylor, Sidney Poitier, Angela Davis, Ella Baker, and so many others. It was like she was hearing these stories for the first time. She wanted to break through to a society who judged her father solely for his skin tone and not his medical degree that he so desperately clung to.

The right side of Blair's brain woke up. She was analytical. Methodical, even. She had been this way for so long that when she got a taste of melanin; she knew she was starved. Her thirst for all things Black was deep-rooted and needed. She read books and joined protests. Her hair that Mrs. Trinidad so carefully permed and pressed faithfully every two weeks during her childhood was replaced with Bantu knots, then later—Sister locks. Blair's once comfy, casual style was replaced with pointed pieces adorning her body. Ankh tattoos, crystals around her neck, and shea butter on her elbows. Blair wore less makeup. She rolled with just sun and skin these days.

Cinderella had arrived at the ball, and honey-she wasn't going back.

Not that Blair's parents didn't teach her all the things about being Black, but they were still old school. *"Don't make White folk mad, they don't like to think you're smarter than them,"* they warned. Her parents were so old school and so brainwashed by American society — they taught their daughter to be *good enough* for White people. They taught her to demand an opportunity at *their* table, and when she finally got that opportunity, she had to be better than them. Blair just wanted to build her own table. The thought scared her as much as she knew it would scare her parents if they were still alive. Nonetheless, she carried on.

Blair wondered why Mr. and Mrs. Trinidad so animatedly discussed the stock market and other important but not-so-important things. Yet, when it came to Blair's skin tone, the conversation became a cautionary tale of survival about how to beat them at their own game. Blair didn't want to beat them. She just wanted to create her own path and something that would last. For her, that started first with a strong foundation and family.

Blair's phone beeped again. This time it was a text from Nana.

Nana: *Talked to Cocina's counselor at the program. She can receive visitors starting this week.*

She puffed some more before her phone screamed at her from her Bluetooth speakers and interrupted her thoughts. She looked at the caller ID. *Ms. Margaret.* Blair had talked her up. She didn't have the mental space right now, so she let the phone ring. Besides, she was a little . . . uhh — lifted. She would call her back later. Ms. Margaret and Blair talked after Carter's last session. He still wasn't talking, Blair shared with Ms. Margaret. At least not to her.

"They often try to label little Black boys. They give them diagnoses which follow them for life. ADHD, impulse disorders, Oppositional Defiant Disorder. I'm not saying those things aren't real, but a lot of times, I believe for our little Black children, trauma would be the better explanation. So many things look like mental health disorders but can be better explained by examining their trauma."

Ms. Margaret gave Blair pamphlets to take home and read. Blair perused them and noticed some things she read sounded a lot like Khalil and Cocina. That part scared her.

"'For some people, if you've experienced anything traumatic in your lifetime, it affects you as you get older. It can affect every aspect of your life, including your health, how you cope with stress, how you feel about others, and how you feel about yourself. Trauma affects everything," Ms. Margaret explained.

Blair thought about Khalil's stomachaches and headaches. Cocina always seemed to be sick, and Carter always sniffed and sneezed around the house. Carter jumped at anything that was loud. And the food.

That was still an issue.

No matter how much food they gave him, no matter how much they told him he could eat, he would still hide it in his room.

"His behaviors are normal. I understand it's turning the whole house upside down. But the best thing that's going to help him right now is consistency, honesty, and love. He needs to know you're not leaving him, and you're not going anywhere. He needs to know that you guys are going to stay, where others have walked out. Most of his life was spent with people walking away from him. That's a scary feeling for a kid; there are still certain things we know nothing about, things that Carter may never share with us. Our job is to be there for the things he says and prepare for the things he might not say. He might not talk for a while, and he may just wake up one day and start talking your ear off and never shut up. We just don't know which way it will go. Everything he's experiencing right now will take time. I'm sorry, Blair, but there's nothing we can do except wait and be there for him," Ms. Margaret professed.

Blair sat alone in her car, lifted, and watching the water. She still wouldn't give up on her family, and she certainly wouldn't give up on Carter. She rubbed out the last small piece, and she started her car. She exited the park and ride area and headed towards Sycamore Street.

CHAPTER 16

Phoenix

November ushered in more unseasonable coldness. With the frigid air came foreboding, cool feelings. The ladies were on their own today: Phoenix, Blair, Raven, Cocina. They were in Mississippi for the day, visiting Cocina at her inpatient program. The ladies agreed that Carter wasn't ready to see his mom, and Khalil, well — he didn't say much of anything. He made a grunting noise when Phoenix asked if he wanted to come. With no decisive answer from him, the ladies went alone.

Phoenix looked around at her family and wondered how they had arrived at that point. She had sat nervously the entire ride, hoping no one noticed her quietness. Her heart was beating so deeply in her chest she felt it booming in her ears. She tried to concentrate on her breathing, and every time she thought she had it under control, they would pass a highway marker, inching them closer and closer to their destination. To Cocina, Phoenix's youngest child. This would be the day, she had decided. The day she would tell her family her story. Phoenix thought about Khalil. She didn't want to tell this story twice, not when she had spent so many years forgetting things. She battled her own memory, which seemed hellbent on remembering it all these days.

Phoenix just wanted to forget. Not because she was running from it, but because she didn't want to look back. What was the point in looking back? Phoenix had gone to counseling as an adult and thought she had done well for herself. Hell, she was dating a White man. If that wasn't proof, she was doing the work she didn't know what was.

Phoenix wasn't a victim; she was a survivor. She had never even seen herself as a victim and wouldn't go down that rabbit hole. Just someone some shit happened to — but shit happened to everyone. Right? But her children — her children, had suffered. And for that, Phoenix would tell this story twice if she had to. *There werejust certain things Khalil and Cocina needed to know,* Phoenix thought on their drive up to Mississippi.

Now sitting before her family at their destination and surrounded by those she loved most in the world, Phoenix felt too intimidated to share. But her family needed to heal, so she took uneven breaths and began to talk.

Phoenix Harris was before her time. If she was guilty of anything, it was being ready for a world that wasn't ready for her. She was born to a hard woman named Elise Harris. Elise was a quiet woman. A subservient woman. A pushover. At least that's what Phoenix thought of her mother. Elise was White. The prettiest White woman in the world to Phoenix, not that she met too many White women — her world was otherwise, pure chocolate back then. She told people that Elise was Creole, at least, that brought her some solace. But Elise wasn't Creole, she was one hundred percent a White woman. Phoenix was the only child born to her parents, Elise, and Duke. Elise was smart and knew how to charm people. She charmed her way into being a secretary even after she flunked out of college. And Duke — well, he worked in a factory. A chicken coop on the outskirts of town where all the guys straight out of high school worked and toughed it out with no other options. Elise and Duke met one day when her Buick took its last breath and hissed to a halt in front of Duke's family's house. The car smoked as she stepped out and slammed the door shut, annoyed. Duke spotted her from the stoop and was slow to help at first. An annoyed White woman could be dangerous for a Black man.

Duke walked towards Elise slowly, not knowing what to expect. She smiled when she saw him. She didn't see color — but rather a man who looked like he could help her. Elise batted her eyes, threw her head back, and laughed too hard at Duke's jokes. She showed all her teeth. She bit on her fingers in her mouth and toyed with her hair as she gave her best damsel in distress performance. It only took thirty minutes for Duke to fix Elise's car, but within that thirty minutes, the path had been laid, and the course of their lives would change forever.

They left together that night, and they shared food and each other's bodies for three glorious days holed up in a motel room. Elise didn't go to work for those three days — but Duke did, arriving each day late and high off Elise's love. Then Elise was *late*.

Elise's family were card-carrying members of the KKK and had Confederate flags plastered everywhere. Everyone from out of town was a Yankee. What would they do if they found Elise, one of their own, sleeping with a Black man? And had the audacity to flaunt it in their face and get pregnant by him?

Elise couldn't risk it. She could be killed.

She made a quick decision she thought would appease both sides. Elise worked hard for nine months to conceal her pregnancy, letting out her dresses a little each week, so they hung loose in the places where her widening hips were swollen. In her ninth month, she visited the local library, where she checked out a book about Greek mythology. She learned about the Phoenix: The bird was associated with the sun and being able to rise from ashes to reclaim a new life. The Phoenix's large protectful wings made Elise feel powerful. She carried a secret that no one knew, only this secret grew and grew until it screamed to be let loose. She never placed her hand to her stomach to feel the baby kicking, she didn't want to get too attached. Elise knew what she had to do and why she had to do it.

In 1961, in Marianna, Arkansas, Elise gave birth to her one and only child, Phoenix Harris — on a quiet April day. She was grateful that it was an easy birth, and she didn't have to ask her boss for any time off from work. Her life never stopped, and Duke didn't care either way. Elise always made it sound like she had things under control, and this was something he didn't have to worry about. So, he didn't.

Elise gave birth to Phoenix and left her with Elise's best friend, Ms. Chrissie. Ms. Chrissie raised Phoenix from the moment she was born. She was an obese Black woman and had trouble moving around her home without help. Ms. Chrissie instructed Phoenix every day from the couch where she slept and lived.

"Turn the water down some more, Phe Phe, I can see it boiling from here," Ms. Chrissie said,

"Never buy a man shoes as a gift, he'll walk away from you with those same shoes on," she would say with a finger point and cigarette hanging out of the corner of her mouth.

"Come here, let me braid your hair, baby girl."

She would sit between Ms. Chrissie's large legs as she braided her hair. Ms. Chrissie delicately parted Phoenix's mane and greased her scalp. One hand behind the other with grease stuck to Ms. Chrissie's hand, she dabbed and braided, dabbed, and braided. They talked about everything. In those moments, Phoenix felt safe.

What Ms. Chrissie lacked in flexibility, she made up for with love, showering Phoenix with knowledge, care, and compassion. Phoenix cooked and cleaned day after day and year after year; she took care of Ms. Chrissie, and Ms. Chrissie took care of her Phe Phe.

Elise came to visit on the weekends from wherever she now lived. Not only had Elise dropped off Phoenix to Ms. Chrissie, but she moved almost six hours away from Phoenix. Elise had given Phoenix and Ms. Chrissie a million reasons the move would benefit them all. Phoenix was seven years old when she realized she didn't care. She had kissed her mom and turned back to Ms. Chrissie, never asking another question about it. She hated those trips when Elise came to visit anyway. She didn't come to spend time with Phoenix, she came to spend time with Duke. Elise would come to Ms. Chrissie's every other weekend, and she would cook fried chicken, corn, and mashed potatoes for Duke, who also came to visit. She would feed him first. Once he cleared his plate, Elise would wash it and put it away. Only then would she feed Phoenix. Sometimes she sat with her and asked her questions. Other times she was off with

Duke, where they laughed and giggled in a different part of the house. She and Ms. Chrissie continued in their own world where only the two of them existed.

Phoenix would look out the window. As much as she loved Ms. Chrissie, she waited and prayed that someone would come and rescue her. She knew this wasn't normal for a kid. She was a smart girl, and she had seen parents at school with her friends, and she noticed a few things. Their moms weren't White, and their moms were always there, not just visiting on the weekends. Phoenix didn't feel like an abused child. She knew about those kids; she had seen them in school too. She wasn't an abused child. Elise and Duke just didn't care about her. She was in their way, the thing that held them back. If it wasn't for her, they could be happily together somewhere, sharing their interracial love where it was allowed — or tolerated, depending on where they went. Even if Elise and Duke would part ways, they would just chalk it up as a summer fling. If they could, they would. Those were just fleeting thoughts because Phoenix was right there, and she kept them tethered to each other. So, they came to see their daughter every other week, to eat fried chicken, corn, and mashed potatoes in their room, and giggle behind closed doors.

One day when Phoenix was thirteen years old, someone rescued her.

It was Elise.

Elise told Phoenix that her grandparents had passed away the week prior. She told her to pack her things because they were moving to Lake Lacroix, where she had bought a house.

Lake who? What was this woman up to now? Phoenix probed.

That was the first time she learned just how selfish her mother was. Phoenix's dad wasn't coming either, Elise mentioned — not that he cared too much anyway. Phoenix went to his house to say goodbye. It was the first time she had ever been there. She found the address a while back when she snooped through Elise's things. She was too afraid to go to Duke's house, but now that they were moving, she wanted to see what his other life was about.

It angered her to learn that her dad lived three blocks from her and Ms. Chrissie. She knocked on the door with the address written in her hand. It took a while for anybody to answer the door, but Phoenix was sure she had the current address. She studied the numbers and address for days.

Someone opened the door who looked like a female version of her Dad. *A sister? Aunt maybe?* Phoenix couldn't see into the house, but she made out more faces, all looking like Duke and even herself in some ways. When Duke laid eyes on Phoenix knocking on the door, his eyes were enormous.

"Is Duke home?" Phoenix asked.

She knew that he was, she saw him when the woman opened the door. Duke ran to Phoenix and shoved her back on the porch. She stumbled a little, and Duke extended his arm to catch her, so she did not fall. He hadn't been trying to push her. He was trying to close the front door behind them so no one else in the house could see Phoenix.

"What, you need something? You going with ya Ma an'em, right?" Duke asked. He didn't let Phoenix get any words in as he dug in his pocket and handed her a wad of money. *"You be a good girl, you hear?"*

Duke kissed Phoenix's forehead, and she couldn't remember the last time her Dad had embraced her. Duke wasn't even looking at Phoenix, he was looking around at his neighbors who were peeking from their windows trying to figure out who the light-skinned young girl was on Duke's front porch.

Phoenix walked home, knowing it would be a long time before she saw her Dad again. She and Elise would move to a shotgun house in Lake Lacroix, in NOLA's backyard. As they departed for the six-hour drive from Marianna, Arkansas, it occurred to Phoenix that she and her mom had never spent so much time together in the car in her entire thirteen years of life, let alone live together. As they arrived in Lake Lacroix, she studied the neighborhood and the large oak trees. She watched the fisherman at the docks hauling in crates of lobster and crawfish. The men appeared hunched over in pain, but they carried on, moving with precision. They knew what to do with their eyes closed. Phoenix had prayed for a new life, and here it was. She was ready.

Once settled in, Phoenix and Elise did not see eye to eye right from the beginning. They didn't converse right from the beginning. The conversation didn't flow naturally like it would for a mother and child who were already familiar with each other, spending long days and nights together forging a family. They filled their relationship with too many secrets swept under the rug, with Elise hell-bent on keeping them there. Elise treated Phoenix as if they were old friends, and when she responded as such, Elise would pull away, yell, and scream at her. She wouldn't speak to Phoenix for days on end. And when she talked to her, she blamed Phoenix for ruining their relationship and not respecting her. When Phoenix tried to level with her mom, Elise would tell her she was going to send her back to Arkansas, *"With ya Daddy an'em."*

Phoenix resented her every step of the way.

"Did you call Ms. Chrissie today?" Phoenix would ask Elise, already knowing the answer.

"She's fine stop worrying about her. I called her last Friday, hush." Elise would reply.

"Well, can I call Daddy?"

Elise said, *"Do what you want."* She slammed her bedroom door shut as if Phoenix had disrespected her.

Phoenix called her father one time, and he rushed her off the phone. He said that he had to go to work, but Phoenix knew that was a lie. There was too much noise and laughing in the background. She called and interrupted a party, and Duke was too busy to talk. Phoenix knew she wouldn't be calling back.

She and Elise always fussed about men being at the house. Elise enjoyed male company, and she was not afraid to be vocal about her needs. Phoenix often woke up as men "accidentally" walked into her room while they were looking for the bathroom. She felt their eyes on her in the morning when she would get ready for school. She never felt safe. It always went the same way. Elise and some man would come in late one night laughing. Elise's voice was always low and raspy, laced with sensual words reserved for her new lover of the month.

Elise never laughed with Phoenix. Her voice was never laced with anything for her daughter that wasn't filled with curse words and a sharp tongue.

School was a problem. Phoenix was gorgeous with her long, honey-blonde dyed hair and smooth caramel skin. She rarely left the home in Arkansas, so when she got to Lake Lacroix, she hadn't expected having to fight her way home from school. Girls always thought that she believed she was better than them because of her color. That she was trying to steal someone's man. Phoenix would have to walk through groups of girls calling her an Oreo and a Skunk. She was in the bathroom at school one day, and when she came out, a group of girls jumped her with a knife. They sliced her forearms when she put her hands up to shield her face. When Phoenix's principal, Mr. Paterno, called Elise and told her what happened, Elise acted as if she was too bothered to even listen to Phoenix's side of things.

She went down to the school to speak on her daughter's behalf, which put them in a public situation, and those always made Elise uncomfortable. Elise was White and Phoenix, well she could pass for either side — which wasn't the right side for Elise. Elise cut her eyes at Phoenix, who sat in the office while blood dripped from her forearms, which were wrapped in the school's toilet paper to help stop the bleeding.

While talking to Mr. Paterno, Elise put on her low and sensual voice that she used with the men who came by their house. Elise used her Whiteness as a shield that day. She sat as her daughter's arms bled in the office, and she flirted with the principal. Elise explained to Mr. Paterno that Phoenix was still adjusting to Lake Lacroix and didn't mean to make any trouble.

Elise shifted her weight and batted her eyes at him as she offered to explain more over coffee. Mr. Paterno had been one of those men, too, leaving out of her mother's bedroom early one morning, with his coat jacket over his arm and hat in his hand — pretending not to peer at Phoenix on his way out.

As Phoenix spoke and shared her story with her family, Raven shifted in her seat. Raven had never, ever heard her grandmother discuss her childhood. Blair was also immersed in Phoenix's words, but for a different reason. Blair knew that if she could empathize with Phoenix, it would help her learn what her husband needed. What Khalil needed.

Phoenix took a sip of water and swallowed hard. She continued talking to her family....

Phoenix and her mom disagreed so much at home that one day, they just stopped communicating. It just seemed easier that way. No one resented the other. No one was walking on eggshells. Phoenix lied about her age and got a job at Roy Rogers. She saved every single penny until she could rent herself a room in a motel at fifteen years old. She only lived with her mom for two years out of her entire life. Phoenix rose, just like the bird she was named after — and rescued herself.

"Everything after that was gravy," Phoenix shrugged. She grabbed a tissue and dabbed large tears from her eyes. All the memories she tried to forget hit her all at once, but she pressed on....

Phoenix met Courtney one day in the Roy Rogers drive through as she was taking his order. There wasn't anything particularly spectacular about him. He whipped around the corner with Whodini "The Freaks Come Out at Night," blasting and weed smoke billowing out the windows. His mouth was full of gold teeth.

She was turned off by him, but out of sheer boredom — she gave him her beeper number. Nine months later came Khalil, and one month after that, a wedding happened when Phoenix was just sixteen years old. She lied about her age again, this time to get married.

Phoenix was determined to be a better mom than she had growing up. She pushed Khalil to be the best and do the best. He played every sport as a child and did all the things she never did. Six years later, Cocina arrived. Courtney thought it would be funny to name her Cocina because that was where she was conceived. Phoenix didn't object. To her, it wasn't worth the fight. While life pressed on around them, Courtney did nothing. Nothing.

Had Phoenix been paying attention, she would have seen Duke. He was written all over Courtney, but hindsight was always 20/20. Courtney sat on the couch all day and night watching TV and drinking beer. He never worked and didn't leave the house. He never seemed interested in the children unless they were in trouble for something.

Phoenix would often get mad, and they would argue. She would scream at him, *"You're not a father, you're just a man that had some kids. And how many are there!?"* He would get mad and, on that note, leave the house. He returned a few hours later, smelling of more beer. Only this beer didn't smell like beer from their home. This beer smelled like beer with a hint of Jasmine perfume from somewhere. So, they argued about that too. Sometimes things got physical. Sometimes Khalil had to break it up. Then sometimes, Courtney would turn the beatings on to Khalil because Khalil dared defend his mom.

There were a lot of sometimes.

Khalil and Cocina's parents did this for years until one day, Courtney died right there in that chair he loved so much. Khalil was eighteen when his father passed away. Cocina was twelve. For the Jamison family, it was an ordinary day with a quickie funeral to save face. No one said it, but with the death of Courtney — the family had been reborn.

Phoenix spoke throughout the session, speaking her truth. She tried to pay special attention to her family as they listened to her, but it was hard to see and hear through her sobs. Phoenix talked, but the inpatient staff ended their session.

"All visits have to end early. We're short staffed tonight, we're so sorry," they said.

The ladies all sighed at the intrusion.

Blair demanded to speak to the administrator on duty, at which time they were promised an additional hour for their next session — but this one would have to be cut short. Phoenix, although she didn't get the reaction, she was looking for, felt lighter. She came into the meeting feeling like she was underwater with weights on. There was always something holding her back and attaching itself to her. Today, sharing her story with her family made her spirit feel settled.

As they escorted Cocina back to her room, she thought about her mom's words. The hour went by fast, and Cocina knew there was a lot more to the story that didn't end there. Cocina's life had been different after her father died, and that was the part of the story where Phoenix was conveniently interrupted. Cocina already knew that ending, though; she had lived it all too well. Regardless, she was happy to hear her mom's words.

CHAPTER 17

They sat there. Shoulder to shoulder.

His bare arm touching Raven's. They were hunched over a sea of equations and sequences. His eyebrows were furrowed, deep in thought. He clicked and clacked on the calculator, and he brought a ruler and graph paper. Raven studied his face without him noticing — at least Raven didn't think he noticed.

21Savage played in the background. The music echoed throughout her room, and the curtains blew from the open window. It was a cool Thursday afternoon, and things were calm in the Jamison household. Amir and Raven crunched numbers for their chemistry project while Khalil waxed his car in the garage. Blair ran errands, and Carter was with his therapist.

"I forgot to tell you; I ran into your Nana at the grocery store the other day." Amir's mouth slightly turned up. He was trying not to smirk.

"Oh yeah, what did she say?"

"Ain't you that lil chocolate boy that be at my Raven's house?"

"What's yo sign?"

"where eyo Mama at?"

"Let me meet her."

"Who y'al people an'em?"

"What time were you born?"

"Okay, okay!" Raven giggled. Amir continued to use Nana's high-pitched voice and roll his neck. They cracked up laughing. Nana was so crazy; she didn't even mention she saw Amir the last time Raven saw her.

It was true.

She and Amir had been spending more time together. She once was awestruck by his beauty, but now she felt settled. Amir brought a calmness to her life. Somewhere over the past few months, they became friends. He liked a few of her pictures on IG. She — a few of his. He liked to post about basketball and what it meant to him, being young and Black in America. He was bold like that.

Raven recorded dance videos of herself imitating Ciara and Teyana Taylor. Amir began tagging her in posts, sending her motivational quotes here and there.

They exchanged numbers, and the conversation moved from social media to texting. She told him a little about herself. Then a lot about herself. Amir told her about his dad — he was doing time in Angola. Locked up for a crime he didn't commit, depending on who you asked. But an uncaring, White jury saw it differently.

Amir just saw a dad. His dad. The dad who put the first basketball in his hands and taught him how to play the game.

And then taught him how to play the game behind the scenes so he could play *their* game.

Amir told her of his many cousins and aunts and uncles in NOLA. He told her of cookouts, card games, birthday parties, Sunday school, and many family events that she had never experienced. It was ironic to her that she lived with both parents all her life, and Amir, by the standards of no one important, came from a broken family. But still — Raven never experienced a sense of family and closeness the way he described it. She and Amir talked about basketball and his love for the game. He was nervous about getting into college. He felt it was his duty to take care of his family. No one told him that directly, but he felt it. His words made her think about lots of things. Along the road, they slipped into a friendship. An easy friendship, a quiet friendship. No pretenses, no confusion. A sense of knowing they were there for each other.

She pondered their friendship as she heard the doorbell ring and voices. Raven couldn't make out the voices, so she shushed Amir. Raven heard a woman.

"Is Carter home?"

Aunt Cocina. She was here in the flesh.

Raven jumped up from her desk and took large steps across her bedroom. She swung her door open, and for the second time in three months, she stood at the top of the hallway steps with bated breath. This time with a few visitors. Cocina and Amir.

"No. He's out with his therapist." Khalil was wiping oil from his hands on a dishrag. Raven couldn't make out his face from the back, but he stood sternly. Mom would be pissed about the dishrag.

"Can I talk to you for a second?" Aunt Cocina shifted her weight to the other leg and noticed the company watching from the top of the steps. Raven smiled, and her aunt nervously smiled back.

"Follow me." Khalil's jaw was a little tighter than Raven had hoped to see.

Amir and Raven followed behind and stood in the kitchen. Khalil ushered Aunt Cocina into the sunroom. Raven figured she probably should give them some privacy, but Khalil didn't tell her to stand down, and she wasn't about to — not yet at least. Both walked in single-file lines with their shoulders slumped. They both had the same walk.

Like relatives. Like, brother and sister.

"I was in rehab." she blurted as Khalil sat down. He stayed silent.

"I-I-I couldn't call. That night, I lost my phone. The cops ripped Carter from me and put him in a car. I . . . I went to rehab. I finished. I finished the whole thing."

This wasn't news to Raven. Raven, Blair, and Phoenix went to visit Aunt Cocina once more at her program, and they knew she was getting out soon. She asked them not to tell Khalil yet. They agreed to keep Cocina's secret, but now she was kicking herself for agreeing to it. The look on Khalil's face told her that he did not find the visit endearing. Amir was breathing deeply next to Raven, his eyes glued to the situation unfolding before them. It was like driving by a car accident, and Amir got a front-row seat to their family drama — again. Raven still scowled about the Voodoo Festival.

"I've been working myself. I'm staying with my sponsor. I'd like to see Carter." Cocina's words were short. She looked nervous but strong at the same time. Khalil still hadn't said a word. "And I want to say thank you for taking care of him . . . You are always there. So, thank you. . . And Blair too. And you. . ." She looked up at Raven, saying each word carefully.

Raven was proud of her Aunt in that moment. She didn't know why, but she was. She could hear Khalil inhale deeply and then hold his breath. He still said nothing.

"Of course, Aunt C." Raven cleared her throat, which was conveniently dry. "Of course, you can see him." *Ugh, where was Mom? She was so good at these things,* she stewed.

"Cocina. No. Just no." Khalil rose from the couch. "Tell me how this time is different? Tell me how we know you are for real this time? Carter is going through the damn ringer. You know he still doesn't sleep at night? Blair has to go in every night and rock him to sleep. And that's only when he lets her! I work my ass off to hold this house together, and, where were you? In rehab, finding yourself, right?! It's been months, CoCo!"

His words stung Raven's soul. They were real, and they were raw. They sounded vile, leaving his lips, and lingered in the air, heavy with regret. Raven was powerless to stop them, and she didn't know how. This was between a brother and sister, something she knew nothing about.

"I had to save myself, Lil. I-I had to go away so I could be better for him. Like you did."

"Don't even compare me going to college to you raising your son! I had to leave CoCo! I had no other choices, and you know that. I had to —"

"Be better!" Khalil and Cocina said in unison.

Raven's breath was caught in her throat, and she couldn't speak. She and Amir still stood arm to arm, only now Amir's arm felt chilly beside hers. The last words left each of their lips at the same time. They left to *be better*. They both said it, but for some reason, they sounded so different. So many other words left unsaid as they stood face to face, squaring off. Brother to sister — the same face. How would they move past this? So many questions lingered in the air. Khalil was unsure if he could let it go. Cocina was unsure if she wanted to or if it was worth it.

"K. Cocina."

Raven finally exhaled as she heard her voice.

Her mom was home.

"I'm so happy that you are here." Blair stood in the doorway, struggling with the grocery bags. Her eyes roamed Cocina's body. Blair looked for the same things Khalil and Raven looked for when Aunt Cocina descended on the front stoop. Track marks, glossy eyes. Blair saw none. Raven and Khalil had seen none.

Blair's eyes softened. "You look well."

"I would like to see Carter," Aunt Cocina faced Blair, gearing up for round two.

"He would like that." Blair shook her head. "Actually, we have a family session Thursday with Carter's therapist. How about you come too? It'll be here at the house. Six o'clock?"

Aunt Cocina's shoulders softened.

"I'll be here." She looked directly at Khalil and walked to the front door. Aunt Cocina stopped next to my dad and placed her hand on his shoulder.

"Thanks, Lil. For everything."

She shut the door behind her.

Blair glanced at Amir with interest. .. "And you are?"

CHAPTER 18

Rain poured outside, and the sounds echoed through the hallways. Raven couldn't believe the weather lately; it was so unusual these days. But then again, so was everything else in her life. Raven was surly.

It was four o'clock Thursday afternoon, and she impatiently waited for the rest of the dance team to arrive. It seemed the rain delayed them. Raven glanced around the gym, feeling the heat rise to her temples. She had other places to be too — but she made it to practice on time. This was her baby, and as Erykah Badu so eloquently put it, "I'm sensitive about my shit."

Raven heard laughter make its way closer and closer until it stopped at the gymnasium doors. Taylor swung it open with Nia and a few other girls walking in together. Nia was in the front, and Taylor and the rest of the betrayers in the back. *Did Nia walk in with them? Like together? As in sharing a conversation and having fun . . . together?*

Raven's eyes darted between the two, staring at each of them. The girls stopped laughing as soon as they laid eyes on Raven, and that told her everything she needed to know. She wanted to practice a new piece by Ciara. She downloaded the video on her phone and wanted to show the girls so they could practice today. This made her switch gears.

"Taylor," Raven sneered. "This is the second time you've been late. I think you should be carpeted."

Taylor was talking to Annalise, and the other girls darted in different directions to the locker room. Nia stayed. Taylor turned towards Raven, confused. 'Carpeted' meant she was restricted from performing that week, essentially sitting on the carpet as her team performed without her.

Raven repeated, "This is the second time you've been late, and according to the bylaws as the team captain, I'm allowed to sit you out one week. So, you're carpeted."

"Are you fucking serious right now?" Taylor's lips turned up at Raven.

"I'm absolutely serious."

Nia stayed at Raven's side. She said nothing, but her eyes fixed on Raven.

"You can't do this," Taylor hollered. "I'm going to Ms. Adams."

Taylor grabbed her things and rushed into Ms. Adams's office at the back of the gym. They could see Taylor flailing her arms and pointing at Raven. Ms. Adams sat in her chair eating a donut and listening. She rose from her seat, wiping powder from her face, and the swish of her tracksuit made its way towards Raven.

"Raven, honey." Ms. Adams's hands were on her hip. She could still see powder on her top lip. "What's this I hear about you carpeting Taylor this week?"

"You know the rules with Ms. Adams, you make us learn them. She's been late to practice twice now in a row, and according to the rules, I can sit her out for one week. So, I am." Raven yielded the last part like it was a dagger.

"Yes, yes, those are the rules, but is that something you really want to do?" Ms. Adams quizzed.

Raven took a deep breath. The heat was still swirling at her temples. "Yes."

Ms. Adams stared at her. "Okay. Well, I guess that's that. Taylor, you will not be dancing this week, per your team captain. You can suit up again next week. Raven, please come see me after practice is over." Ms. Adams walked back to her office; this time slower.

Taylor glared at Raven, and her eyes meant to kill. She grabbed her gym bag and stomped towards the exit. Raven waited for Taylor to leave before blowing her whistle as the girls ran out of the locker room, pretending not to listen. They were suited up and ready for practice. All of them were late — but Raven had only called out one of them.

Raven opened her phone and swiped away from the Ciara track she wanted to show them. That would have to wait for another day, clearly. She found her NOLA bounce playlist, and she inhaled. This would work. . . the girls didn't dance to NOLA Bounce often; Raven liked to show people they were versatile.

But if there was anything that got them all the way together, it was a bounce beat!

She hit play and synced the music to the gym speakers. Soon, sounds of the drums and trombone could be heard throughout. The girls swayed and vibed while Raven watched.

Raven turned the music louder and stood in front of the team. She rocked back and forth, "That's right, come on. You hear that bass? Let's go, girls," she encouraged. The girls followed Raven's lead as she gyrated and grooved in front of the mirror, staring back at them from the wall.

"Good job Bria arch your back just a little bit more," she yelled over the music. The sound pulsated through the gym. Raven turned to face the group, noticing Taylor missing from the back left corner. The group looked lopsided-uneven, without her. Still, Raven didn't miss her presence, not even for dance.

Once the music ended, Raven avoided Nia's eyes, and she dismissed the team. "Good job today." She waved to the girls, towel in hand.

Nia ran to grab a bottle of water, and Raven darted off in the opposite direction, ducking out of the back door. She would not be staying after to talk to Ms. Adams today either.

CHAPTER 19

Khalil

"Hi Mr. Jamison, this is Mrs. Johnson from Lake Lacroix Elementary calling regarding Carter. He tore apart the classroom again. We had a fire drill, and Carter lost it. Cursing and screaming. We need you to come pick him up now. We should also discuss school placement options for the future."

"Yes. Okay. Yes." Khalil spoke robotically on the phone. He did a U-turn in his police car, heading toward Carter's school.

Khalil banged his hand on the steering wheel as he drove.

It was all her fault. Everything was her fault, he moped. Khalil had been thinking about his life and where things had gone wrong. Phoenix seemed to be the common denominator here.

Khalil stewed, but he knew that wasn't entirely fair or even true. He wiped his face with his hand and glimpsed himself in the rearview mirror. He was just at the school last week for a community event, and now he was back, picking up Carter after they kicked him out.

My, how things change, he lamented.

Khalil thought about his own parents and childhood. Whatever kind of abuse you can name, it was there. His parents refused to throw in the towel, and they stayed together no matter what. There was a lot of *whats*. Not for love, but because they shared the same toxic behaviors. Domestic violence was okay, as long as the kids didn't see. The lights and gas would get shut off, and that too was okay — everyone ran out of money at the end of the month.

Khalil's parents shared the same scarcity mentalities that held Black people back for so long. The man gets abused at work by Bossman, comes home, and takes it out on his wife; then she takes it out on the kids. They grew up in dysfunction, and Khalil knew right from the beginning it was no way to grow up. He was never there for Cocina. His parents were never there for him.

Co-Co and I didn't stand a chance, he mused.

Phoenix pretended this part of her life didn't happen, but he vividly remembered her having a full-time relationship with Jack Daniels. And Courtney did his best to discipline the kids so the bruises wouldn't show.

I got out, Khalil thought. *I left.* He loved his family, but he knew it wasn't healthy for him to keep them in his life.

When he left the home, Cocina was only twelve. He turned eighteen and put as much distance between him and his family as he could. He and Cocina spoke now and then when he would call to check in. Mom would be drunk, and Dad sounded miserable and surly — per usual.

"What now, Boy? Don't call here begging for no money. You a big-time college boy, you don't need us," Courtney spewed. After a while, his Dad wouldn't even greet him when he called. He handed the mounted walk phone off to Cocina.

"*Yes. School is fine. Mom is fine too. Dad is fine."* Cocina sounded mechanical. Almost programmed. Having lived in that household, he knew that feeling all too well. Khalil felt their distance physically and emotionally. Eventually, he stopped calling all together. He heard from CPS a few years later Cocina was in foster care.

"Physical abuse allegations — substantiated," a woman read to him from a file over the phone. The woman put him on hold twice — and she munched on potato chips when she told Khalil his baby-sister was in foster care, light years away. He knew what that meant without knowing what it meant. He had a dorm room, and although he couldn't take her in, he still felt guilty. This was a cross he would bear the rest of their lives. Cocina reminded him of their past. Harder times. Pain, tears, and strength he didn't know he needed to have at five years old, then ten years old, then fifteen.

Khalil thought about his wife. Had he isolated himself? Pushed her away and inadvertently made her the default parent? So many questions ran through his mind while comparing himself to Courtney. Khalil had no good memories of his dad. He wasn't sure if he blocked them out or if the easier answer was there simply no good memories to recount. Going away to college had been the best thing that happened to him at that time. He met many people, but he didn't see enough to keep him there. College hadn't been some grand, life-changing experience for him like it was for other people. No one told him how to be a college student. Or taught him about financial aid. There was no career counselor to walk him through the experience. So, he struggled there, too, and eventually dropped out. He didn't see himself as a college career type of guy, anyway. He wanted to speak up for the little guy — so that's what he did. He left Tulane University and never looked back. He knew his place in life would not be confined to those four years, so he did the next best thing.

Khalil joined the police academy, where he was proud. Established. He was about that cop life. He enjoyed making connections with the community and going to Raven's school when they needed to do "Coffee with a Cop" events. He wore his uniform with a sense of fulfillment. Lake Lacroix's police department was predominantly Black, and to him — that meant everything. Patrolling and protecting his own community was a tall order, which he intended to manage to the best of his abilities. *But look at what was left behind,* another voice countered in his head.

Cocina.

When Khalil's trusted colleagues began whispering about his family and making jokes about Cocina, his blood would boil. He didn't like confrontation, but he also wasn't there to be disrespected either. Khalil would address those who had the most to say in their own time, but first, he had to make changes within himself.

Why did Cocina have so many issues which made her the talk of the town? Had he helped her the best he could, or did he turn a blind eye to save himself? Khalil understood it at that moment. It was as if something had clicked. Blair was killing herself to hold things together while he ran. He laughed it off. Carter affected the entire household, and while they committed everyone to doing their part — Khalil skipped out, hiding behind work. He intended to be a different man, a better man than his father, but now he saw that he was just running. He was so angry for so long.

It wasn't like Phoenix didn't try to make amends. Khalil was short-tempered whenever the topic of their childhood came up. She tried a few times to have that conversation, but he shut it down. They didn't need to talk about it; they had gotten through it and survived. The conversation wasn't needed.

Oh, but it *was* needed.

Phoenix had dropped the conversation and didn't broach the subject again with Khalil. He tried to be strong and take on anything, but somewhere deep in him needed a hug from his mom. And yet, here they were. Years later, Carter experienced some of the same things that Khalil experienced as a child. This made his chest tight.

Khalil felt a sense of urgency. This time was different, and they all knew it. Khalil had to step up more and not idly sit back like Courtney had. He stared at himself once more in the mirror. He shut his police vehicle off and walked inside.

Khalil retrieved Carter from school, and they drove home in silence, both deep in thought. Khalil watched so many families at the station. Older generations of terrible parents. Paying the price for their younger choices by having to raise their grandchildren. So many aunts, uncles, cousins, stepping up and fulfilling roles they never intended. Stepping up when others walked out. This was his role now. Stepping up when Cocina ran out. Stepping up when Cocina couldn't be bothered to parent.

Khalil's disappointment was heavy. It clung to him like his police uniform he so proudly wore. Now it felt tight.

Khalil swallowed. "Carter, I'm at a loss here. I-I- don't know what to do." "Why do you hate me?" Carter interrupted. His hands cradled in his lap. He didn't look up as he spoke. Khalil's eyes widened at Carter's words.

"I don't hate you." Khalil's voice cracked.

"I'm just worried. About you. Your mom. . ." Khalil found it so easy to talk to the kids at the station. But why did he struggle to find the words with Carter? "I've failed you, I'm so sorry, Carter." He struggled to find the words but pressed on. He didn't have a joke or something to lighten up the mood.

"You know, when me and your mom were kids, she was always beefing with someone. Even at a young age, we always caught her in some drama."

Carter's eyes twinkled. He had heard no family stories of his mom's childhood.

"She used to pick fights with people and then run all the way home. She never got into a fight, but damned if she didn't start every single one. I mean, you think Usain Bolt is fast, you should've seen your mama with three or four people chasing her down the streets-sometimes dogs too! I mean knees to chest, booking it down the street. She would run all the way home and get me. I was young. . ." Khalil chuckled. He remembered it vividly.

"I had to come outside and fight. Every week, it would be someone new or some issue that she had, and every week I had to fight to defend her." "Did you win the fights?" Carter's eyes were wide.

"I sure did. Every single one." Khalil grinned. This news seemed to please Carter, and he nodded his head.

"Your mom used to call me a Black RoboCop." Khalil and Carter laughed in unison, surprising each other. "Then she would just call me her cop. You know, it was her who made me believe I could be a cop in real life." Khalil carefully chose his words. "Carter, you will win all the fights too. Every single one. You've got a cop on your side too. But you have to tell me what you need, so I know how to help. I don't hate you. You're my nephew, and I love you. I always love you."

Carter sat quietly for a while and then looked at his Uncle Lil. "Nah, I don't mess with Twelve. But I hear you. I hear you, Uncle Lil." Both of them sat with wet eyes, relaxed shoulders, and minds open, staring into the front windshield as they drove home — together.

CHAPTER 20

Raven and Nia sat at Nia's house helping Ms. Tina prepare flyers and compose emails. Ms. Tina was drafting a character reference for Ms. Twizz's son, Ryan, regarding getting his prison sentence reduced.

Nia's dad passed away when she was younger. Raven wasn't sure exactly what happened because Nia didn't talk about it, but Raven overheard Blair whispering to Khalil that he passed away in a car accident when a teen driver hit him. Blair said this was part of the reason Ms. Tina became an Attorney.

Ms. Twizz picked at her fingers while she waited. Ms. Tina walked in with a tray of hot tea for Ms. Twizz and sweet tea for Nia and Raven. The girls took a glass while Ms. Twizz stirred her tea. She remained quiet. Not knowing what to expect, Ms. Twizz brought her entire crate of files, paperwork, and scraps of receipts.

"Let's start here," Ms. Tina got comfortable on the loveseat. "Tell me about Ryan. What do you think is important for others to know about him? What may be helpful for the judge to know? Anything makes his case unique?" Ms. Tina sat her recorder on the table, and she grabbed a notebook and pen.

Ms. Twizz sighed, and her shoulders tightened up. She looked around the room and began. "Well, I had him and his brothers young. I didn't know what I was doing. They daddy came to me, and he said he wanted me, and I was with him now. My self-esteem was so low that I thought I liked him too. I thought that's all it took. They chose you.

"I had so many things happen to me I didn't choose. So, I thought this was how it went — someone chose you, and you belonged to them now. When things happen to girls at young ages, it changes their outlook on men. You expect less because they only want certain things from you, anyway, so why not just give it to them upfront?" Ms. Twizz dabbed at her eyes. "I've always tried to be a good Mom, but I didn't learn how. . . Now Ryan, Ryan, is my youngest. His dad lives in Atlanta, and he's only met him a few times. Ryan's daddy was a drug dealer, and Ryan was a drug dealer. What else is there to say about that? I guess it ran in the family. If my son's skin was a bit lighter, this really would be a different story. But because he's a Black man living in America — he's a criminal, a threat. He got what came to him, they say. No-no, that's not my child. My child likes to cook, and he likes to read. Did you know he can draw? Probably better than some of them folk at your Mama's place," she pointed to Raven. "I have his son, Ryan Jr. RJ lives with me. I want to give big Ryan a chance to be the father he never had. You know, we have to change things for the younger generation." Ms. Twizz leaned into Ms. Tina and whispered, ". . . it's all about them now."

She allowed not one tear to fall. Raven and Nia sat with bated breath as they listened to Ms. Twizz talk. Raven could picture Ms. Twizz's accounts in her head. In some ways, they reminded her of Nana's story. They were Black women who made decisions when they were younger that affected their families going forward. Raven could hear the worry and nervousness in Ms. Twizz's voice and wondered if Nana felt the same way.

"We all just want to make the people that come after us better humans. And that seems to be the hardest thing to do." Her words trailed off. "I can't believe some of the stories big Ryan tells me. Situations I completely forgot about-or I thought the kids didn't notice. They saw, and they noticed. But Ryan and I keep talking anyway, and we keep forging on, and we keep fixin' our relationship. The only thing that's going to help is talking and dealing with it. So that's what we do.

"If Ryan and I can do all that, then I know he'll come around. I feel it. Ryan ain't no bad guy. He ain't no worse than some of these other busters walking around here on the streets now, but he was young — and he deserves a second chance just like all of them other young White boys around the country. They get their second chances when they be raping them little White girls. They get told *'it's okay, we don't want to ruin your future — we'll work with you.'* But you want to ruin my baby's future? No-no. I'm not making no excuses for him. He did his crime. I am saying give my baby a second chance. Don't demonize him for my choices as a parent."

Ms. Twizz sat quietly for a while, thinking. Ms. Tina, Raven, and Nia waited. Ms. Tina turned off the recorder a while ago and was letting Ms. Twizz talk as she and the girls listened.

"Did I ever tell ya'll I used to bake cakes? Big, beautiful cakes. Cupcakes, wedding cakes, birthday cakes, just-because-you-got-you-a-sweet-tooth cake, baby shower cakes, I made them all," her smile was bright. "Everyone in town used to come for some of Ms. Twizz's cakes; they were that good. You know the supermarket Piggly Wiggly? They even came to me one time about selling some of my cakes in the supermarket. That was a good day."

Her eyes were far away... "But I was too busy chasing behind Ryan's daddy. I didn't take myself or my craft seriously. I listened to what they daddy told me and did what he asked me to do. I couldn't even make myself happy, let alone anyone else," she cackled. "He didn't ask me anything when he went and fooled around. He spent all the money and left us to figure out what to do when the lights were off. And the one thing I could do to support my family on my own without him was those cakes. See — at the time, I didn't realize it, but I could've been a Black woman doing it ya'll!" Ms. Twizz slapped her knee with bright eyes. "I was so busy chasing behind him, I didn't recognize my own power— but he did. He didn't nurture it, he didn't honor it, or push me to be the best I could be for our family."

He held me back.

"And he was what stopped me from signing a contract with Piggly Wiggly for my cakes. Because he didn't think it was a good idea. I regret that to this day. To this day. . .. When y'all find something, and y'all's is great at it — like really great — stick with it. Don't let anyone tell you can't do something, especially no man. Because when the chips are falling, you going to have to support you. Make sure you have the means to do that. Don't be listening to no man. Make sure you love you enough to follow your own dreams." Ms. Twizz sat tall.

Raven felt heat all over her body, Ms. Twizz's words tingled in her stomach, and she felt it down to her toes. Raven looked over at Nia, and she was breathing deep, holding on to Ms. Twizz's words just like she was. Raven glanced over to Miss Tina and noticed she had stopped writing.

"And let me tell y'all's something else. Fix your families. I spent too many years away from all my boys, angry at myself for things I had done. I felt so guilty for not being there when I should have been. They were angry at me for things I had done to them. Things that I hadn't given them. Things that I didn't know I needed to give. I didn't know who I was, let alone be somebody's Mama. You ever hear that saying you grow up with your kids? Well, I grew up with my kids. I did." She shook her head.

"But it didn't make them any better. I grew up with them, but I wasn't grown . . . But guess what? When we started talking again, and I became a mom to my boys, there were just as many good memories as bad. Not everything was bad, I can guarantee you that. God picked them people to be your family. You get them because you need them." Ms. Twizz turned to Raven and looked her square in her eyes. "Raven, you need to be a big cousin to that boy. You hear me? You can do better than that. I've noticed you with him. Don't be acting like he's working on your nerves. " He doesn't." Raven grabbed a tissue. "You treat him like he's in the way. That's yo family! Act like it." She said what she said. "And Nia, you let your Mama date now, you hear me, girl? She needs some lovin' too." Ms. Twizz added. Nia and her Mom locked eyes. Nia hadn't told Raven that her Mom was dating. "I like y'all's girls' friendships. Y'all are real. I'm older. I can tell a good friend from a bad friend. I look somebody up and down in ten seconds, and I can tell you, *'that ain't yo friend girl, that ain't yo people.'* But you and your friends, you girls are solid. That's another relationship you don't give up on. When you build a circle of women who protect you and make you better, well, what's greater than support, baby? Keep them around, they your people." Ms. Twizz's head was held high. "Is that everything? Did you get it all?" Ms. Twizz glanced at her watch. "I have to go pick up RJ from his mama house."

They all were dabbing their eyes.

"Yes, I got everything I needed a while ago, Ms. Twizz. I think this is enough to request another hearing," Ms. Tina said.

Raven felt lighter. She couldn't describe it, but Ms. Twizz's words felt like a call to action. She looked at Nia. Her eyes were red too.

"I'll get this typed and have our request submitted to the prosecutor soon. I'll keep you posted."

Ms. Twizz rose from her seat and grabbed Ms. Tina with a bear hug. She held her for a long time as Ms. Tina crumbled in her arms and sobbed.

"No matter what happens, thank you girl, thank you," Ms. Twizz held Ms. Tina.

CHAPTER 21

Jasmine's house was full of noise, and Raven loved going over there most Friday nights. Tonight, it was mandatory that Raven visit.

Jasmine lived with her Dad and two older brothers. Blair told Raven that Jasmine's mom suffered from bipolar disorder, and she lived across town with Jasmine's grandparents. Jasmine seemed embarrassed by her mom; one time, she came to school yelling and cursing, wearing a green wrestling suit and red Jordan's laced all the way up tight, choking her feet. Everyone assumed she had a psychotic break. The school had to call the police, and Jasmine was absent for a few days after that.

Blair seemed to know everything; it was funny how much information ran through an art gallery. She always knew the inner workings of someone's heart, even when she didn't know them at all.

When Jasmine came to Raven's house to hang out, Blair barged into the room using her I'm-a-nice-mom voice with Jasmine. Like she was delicate or something. She was one of Raven's strongest friends, and Raven valued her opinion. Jasmine's family had planned a crab boil tonight, and Raven was ready. Jasmine's brother, Ant, cooked the seafood downstairs, and the aromas of Old Bay, beer, and butter lingered in the air. This was about to be the highlight of a dreadful week.

"Please tell your Nana I'm so serious about her fanny packs. I need to get me a bedazzled fanny pack by Spring Fling," Jasmine modeled in the mirror. The girls fell into a fit of giggles.

"I'll let her know. She's over the house all the time now anyway. . ." Raven said and let it trail off.

Raven's thoughts couldn't escape her. As much as she tried not to think about it, she had word vomit. Just like with Ms. Whitaker, Raven told Jasmine everything. She told her about Carter not sleeping, hiding food, her dad's disappearing acts, her mom holding them all together and trying not to crack. Hot, angry tears fell from Raven's eyes. She was angry about that too — she was tired of breaking down. Tired of worrying. Raven wanted things to go back to the way they were before Carter changed everything. She swallowed that feeling away in the pit of her stomach.

Rome was burning around her, and she was powerless to stop it.

Jasmine sat knitting and listening. Raven watched her fingers weave in and out of the fabrics. Jasmine was the only Black girl Raven knew that knitted for fun.

“Is that to put over my mouth?” Raven gave a forced chuckle.

“Is that what you want to happen?” Jasmine piqued.

Raven thought for a while before answering. “I just want them to be okay.”

“Have you asked Carter what he wants?”

“No, he’s still not really talking. I mean, it’s gotten better. We get a few words here and there. But he’s not talking-talking.”

“Maybe you should ask him. Don’t stop asking. Don’t let up.”

With a sharp inhale, Raven gauged Jasmine’s words. Raven did everything she thought she was supposed to do as a big cousin. She tried being mature, sitting and talking with him, but she got no response. She tried being comical and would poke fun of her Dad and his dancing, but she got no response. No one in the family received more than a grunt, wave, or point when Carter wanted something. Raven figured he wanted to be left alone, so she stopped trying.

Jasmine sat her knitting needle down.

“My mom. She’s bipolar. Like really bipolar. Sometimes she would drive us around on scavenger hunts through NOLA. Everyone said how dangerous she could be and what they thought was best for us. They said we shouldn’t be around her. I wish someone asked me what I wanted instead of assuming. I would’ve just said I wanted my mom.”

Raven held her breath. . Jasmine never talked about her mom. The last time she mentioned her mom, it was after they arrested her for shoplifting. Jasmine mentioned it one day at the Lake. Not to the group, though — she mentioned it to Raven only. Raven noted that and kept her admission between them.

She pondered Jasmine's words. Had she ever tried talking to Carter herself? Or had she tiptoed around him, thinking that's what he needed? Her silence because of his silence. Did he sense Raven's feelings of anger because he disrupted her life? Did she ask him what he needed? The answers hung heavy in Raven's mind because she already knew the answers. Guilt hit her like a wave.

Jasmine continued knitting. "I'm just saying. . . look at yourself, too, everyone plays a role in the family. Right now, you may need to step up more."

Raven felt her face redden. "But I have asked him, I have tried talking to him. . . . You don't get it," Raven turned away.

Jasmine put her needle back down. "I'll tell you what I see. I see you play the victim sometimes. And I say that out of a place of love, Ray. You are not the only one this affects. I've experienced being forgotten, left out because people won't learn how to talk to you. They stop trying. Don't forget about him. He might not be talking, but I bet he's listening."

Jasmine's words hit Raven like a ton of bricks. She was ready to come back at Jasmine with another inconvenience that Carter had caused when she stopped. *What was her role? Did she make things more difficult? Play the victim at other times?* Raven's brain worked overtime now, trying to piece it all together. She knew for sure she left her mom hanging a few times. She ditched her on grocery trips, appointments. Anything which required Carter to come, Raven found a reason to get out of. She was mad with her dad for his lack of presence at home, and yet she isolated herself the same way.

"Talk to him, how, though?" Raven was ashamed to even say those words. Mainly because she didn't know. Raven didn't know how to talk to her cousin. She was also afraid of his words.

"Well, for starters — don't talk to him like he's some victim. No one wants to feel like people have pity for them. Talk to him regular. Start there." Jasmine suggested.

Raven sighed.

"It's not as hard as you're making it out to be. I wish you could see you right now." Jasmine shook her head.

"See me through me? What does that even mean?" Raven's voice cracked.

"It means go talk to your cousin! Stop trying to come for me! You know what you need to do!" Jasmine reasoned. Her knitting needle fell to the floor. She never raised her voice with Raven. She saw Jasmine cut an eye at Nia a time or two, but never was that sharpness reserved for Raven — until now. Jasmine picked her needle off the floor and took a deep breath. Raven noticed a teeny tiny tear in the corner of her left eye. It was so tiny, Raven almost missed it.

"So . . . how's things with your mom now?" Raven asked.

"When she's here, she's here. And when she's not. She's just not." Jasmine knitted slower now. Her eyes looked far away. Those few words made perfect sense to Raven "Y'all come eat!" Ant hollered up to Jasmine and Raven from the bottom of the steps. They turned the music down and heard dishes clinking from downstairs. Jasmine snapped out of her own thoughts and said, "Girl, let's go. I'm starving." Suddenly Raven didn't have much of an appetite.

CHAPTER 22

It was another rainy afternoon, and they were studying in the school library. Amir was his usual upbeat self, and they sat across from each other, sharing a table for two. Amir was face down in a book, and Raven was staring out of the window. He scrunched his face at her, and he even texted her a funny meme, but nothing seemed to jar Raven out of her thoughts.

“Anything on your mind?” He peeked at Raven from the top of his book. “No. What page are the directions on again? I didn’t see it?”

“Page 330,” Amir said through a tight mouth.

They were testing how to lower the freezing point of water for their chemistry project. Raven was usually excited about all thing’s chemistry, but this time she really couldn’t get with it. Amir was carrying them for most of the project. She was unsure why they were even partners; she was clearly dead weight.

Raven ruminated in her thoughts and felt Amir’s eyes on her. “What?” Her cheeks were hot.

“Raven, focus.” His voice was soft.

She shifted in her seat, hearing his voice change.

Amir closed his book and grabbed his jacket. “Let’s go to the lab.” Raven shrugged her shoulders and followed his lead.

"I heard about what happened with Taylor. . ." They left the library, heading to the chemistry lab. Raven's heart skipped a beat. He knew about her most recent shame. She hung her head lower.

"She came at me. I've never had issues with her, and suddenly she's trying to convince me I posted something about her last year! It wasn't even about her! And I don't know if I should apologize. But we were never friends, to begin with, so how can I apologize?"

She was rambling.

"Ray . . ." Amir said. Hearing him say Ray quieted her. "People go through things others know nothing about. Sometimes it's not about us."

"Yeah, but —"

"Don't take on someone else's drama," he continued. "Don't take ownership of that. If what you said wasn't said with bad intentions, then let it go. You've done all you can."

She wanted to cry again. So many times, these days, she had to blink back tears. This day it was sheer frustration. Raven needed to change this subject. She spent too much time worrying about other people. And besides, she was tired of crying.

"We'll need cups, water, ice, markers, salt, and sugar to make our project," Raven said out loud, looking at the instructions and making sure they had all the materials. Mr.

Fritzel had called it a small but mighty project. Raven didn't think you could get any smaller than water and ice.

She carefully studied the ingredient list and instructions. She went through an entire sleeve of cups, filling them with water and sugar. Raven could never figure out the math part, that's what always tripped her up. She threw out cup after cup of the wrong amounts of sugar versus water. Amir watched her struggling with the water, and he stepped in and took over. Normally she would try to prove she could keep up with Amir, but today she happily did as he instructed. They tested six solutions total, three salt, and three sugar.

"Make sure you rinse and dry the thermometer each time you dip it," Amir said. Raven watched him walking throughout the lab. He was so confident. They went through each aisle, checking beakers and stealing brief glances at each other. When he caught her eye, he quickly turned away. When she stole her own glances, and he caught her — she blushed.

Raven checked the temperature to each beaker in her row, and they now both kept watch. They checked the test tubes frequently during the first five minutes, looking for crystals. After about forty minutes, they saw crystals form. The last beaker seemed to struggle the most, so Amir stood directly in front of that one and watched while she paced back and forth, checking the others.

They continued to study the beakers for some time before Amir whispered, “Oh shit, it worked.”

They were both pleasantly surprised. The opaque, white regions were frozen. They had successfully lowered the temperature of water and froze it using salt and sugar. Raven feverishly walked around, recording the temperatures of each beaker so they could determine if the salt or the sugar worked best and at what temperatures.

“Which one froze first?” Raven quizzed.

“Ummm, four, I believe.”

“You believe?”

“No, I’m sure, it was four. I remember you were standing at number seven, and I was at number four, and I remember looking down and then up at you. So yes, I was at four.” Amir acted out the scenario as if it were a crime scene, and he found the smoking gun.

“You remembered I was standing at number seven? Stalkeeer.” Raven teased.

Amir gave her a sheepish grin, “Shut up!”

Just to be sure, Amir and Raven completed another round and melted the ice for a second time. Raven read the instructions again and handled the glass test tubes as delicately as she could. Amir did the same with the vials on the other side of the lab.

She was looking at Amir when the corner of her jeans hooked onto the lab table. She bumped the ledge, and before she realized it, she dropped glass number four. Glass shards scattered everywhere across the lab floor, and the noise made her jump back and shriek.

"It's okay, it's okay," Amir said, making his way towards Raven and grabbing the mop and broom off the nearby wall. He quickly cleaned up the glass and water that was scattered around them. Raven couldn't find any shards of glass after he was done. "I-I'm sorry. I tripped," she moaned.

"Ray, it's okay. No more apologies, okay? They're not needed. Not with me."

She swallowed the lump forming in her throat.

"Let's start again," she offered. They repeated the process and filled the cups with water, some with sugar and some with salt. They walked around each cup with more ingredients and checked the temperatures. They move in unison, like a team. The mindless work kept Raven's thoughts off other things, and Amir welcomed the conversation. They had no trouble talking about everything, and when there were no interruptions — they could go for hours. Raven and Amir checked the vials again after forty minutes, and sure enough, all six remaining vials were frozen. She copied the numbers in their lab notebook so they could recreate it once again for the big day.

"I see you down there at four!" Raven yelled to Amir. He hunched over the fourth vial, staring at it closely. Raven had jarred him from his own thoughts.

Amir giggled and flung water at her from the other row.

"Ugh! No, you didn't!" Raven squawked, running to fill a styrofoam cup.

Before Raven could make it back, Amir already filled a water bottle and was spraying it at her like a fire hose with his thumb over the lid.

"Ahhh," she shrieked. She ran away from Amir.

He tried to chase her, and they both slipped and slid around the room. They laughed and chased each other. "Cut it out!" Raven yelped with clenched eyes. She was out of breath. She was laughing so hard her voice was raw.

"Nope, I owe you for breaking my ice I worked so hard on!" Amir was now pretending to be an elephant spewing water from his trunk. Raven ducked to slide under Amir and run behind him, but he caught on. He dropped the water bottle from above his head to catch her before she tried to slide under him.

They both slid haphazardly into the wall next to them and stood there catching their breath. They were leaned up against the wall and each other. Raven could taste her conditioner running down her cheek from her wet hair. It burned her eyes, but it was okay. Amir's red Adidas shirt was soaked with water, and Raven could see his abs through his shirt.

She studied his face.

She had studied it before, but somehow it looked different today. It reminded her of chilly nights wrapped under her blanket. It reminded her of her dad walking into the house and her mom greeting him with a *"Hey Lover."* It was Raven's friends always being there for her. She tried to place the feeling, and it didn't take long. She knew what it was immediately. Safe. Amir

made her feel safe. She felt it when she looked into his eyes. Amir held Raven's gaze. But this time, there were no rows, no ice, and no beakers between them to break their stare. They stood leaned up against each other, both panting. Neither of them moved or said a word. It seemed like an eternity passed, but somehow, Raven knew it had only been seconds.

"What is going on in here?" Mr. Fritzel burst into the room and saw water everywhere. "You know what, I don't even want to know, get it cleaned up and go home! The after-school bus will be here soon!" Shaking his head, he left and closed the door behind him. Raven grabbed the broom. She and Amir turned back to each other, this time sharing another laugh.

CHAPTER 23

Raven was lying in bed before school when she heard a loud commotion. She threw her blankets back and ran down the hallway as her feet slapped the hardwood floor. She burst into Carter's bedroom and adjusted her eyes to what she was seeing. Carter was tearing up his room again. Papers, blankets, shoes, and water bottles were flying all over the place. He grunted and tried to move his desk to lift it above his head.

"Carter, Carter, what's wrong?!" She grabbed his arms and noticed the scratches. He pushed her back as she grabbed his shirt collar and ripped it. She toppled over onto his bed. Carter didn't speak but continued ripping things off the walls and flipping his mattress from the floor. He cursed, screamed, and foamed at the mouth. His eyes were dark and crazily rolling in his head. He almost looked unrecognizable.

They tussled for a while with him besting Raven; she didn't realize how strong he was. She felt his heart beating against her own chest. Sweat sat on Carter's brown skin, and he squinted like he expected trouble. Raven wondered how long things that way for him had been, expecting trouble.

"Carter, stop!" Raven screamed as she tried wrestling him into a bear hug. Carter's body went limp with Raven's arms around him, and he slid to the floor and cried. Raven breathed sharply, and she saw stars. She steadied herself against the wall, and they sat on the floor together.

"I'm-I'm sorry." Carter finally said with tears streaking his brown face. "I don't want to go back. Please don't send me back," he said.

"Shhhh shhhh," Raven rocked him.

Raven and Carter sat just like that, and she consoled him. Her leg was cramped, but she didn't move him. Her neck ached, but she pushed through the pain. While she settled Carter, she could hear the school bus pass by — without her on it.

"Did something happen?"

"No, nothing happened. I just do this sometimes." he looked up at Raven. His eyes looked fearful. Worried. There were so many things he didn't say, but his eyes told on him.

"Is she going to take me?"

"I don't know." Raven wiped sweat from her face.

"Is Unc gonna let her take me?"

Raven didn't know. She didn't have an answer for that, but she lied, anyway. "No."

Raven waited so long for Carter to talk, and when he finally did, she had to lie. Well, it really wasn't a lie, she just wasn't sure what was going to happen. She took a deep breath and tried again.

"Do you want to stay?"

He shook his head yes.

"She can come to visit. But I want to stay here," he said matter-of-factly. "Then that's what we'll do."

Carter's body relaxed to those words. She didn't realize his body was so tense in her arms. She didn't know what else to do, so she talked. Raven didn't understand his quietness, but she understood feeling misunderstood — like how Jasmine did. Raven thought about Jasmine in that quiet moment too. She talked for the both, and Carter listened intently, adding in a head nod or a snort when necessary. Raven told him about Ms. Whitaker in school and the things she taught her about calming herself. Raven told him everything she knew about anxiety and how it looks different for everyone. She told him about Ms. Twizz and them trying to get her son out of prison. She told Carter about chemistry class and Amir. They laughed about Nana's Johnny Gil and her fanny packs.

Tears fell from Carter's face as he talked about his mom.

More tears fell from Raven's eyes as she listened.

She admitted her shame about carpeting Taylor. Raven had not shared her innermost thoughts with anyone about the Taylor debacle. Carter had no couth. He peered up at Raven and said, "You were jealous. You thought she was trading on you for Nia." Raven giggled to herself. He was right, she admitted. Soon enough, the sun peeked its head through the clouds. Carter's breathing changed. Raven looked down; he was asleep in her arms.

"Baby girl, you okay?" Khalil asked as he stood in the doorway in his uniform and watched Raven and Carter closely. Khalil peeked into Carter's room, assessing the mess. He didn't say a word about it. Raven's back ached, and her mouth was dry. She and Carter both fell asleep and missed the school bus. Khalil helped Raven move a sleeping Carter out of her arms, and they picked his mattress off the floor, replacing it back into the bed frame. They eased Carter into his bed, and he curled up into a ball and buried himself under the blankets.

"Can you turn the light out?" Carter asked quietly.

Raven and Khalil looked at each other and softly shut the door, clicking the light off.

There would be no school that day.

Later that evening, Carter was ravenous by the time they sat down for dinner. He talked but didn't mention what happened earlier. He seemed different. Blair tripped into the house carrying grocery bags and called them everything but a child of God, and Carter thought it was hilarious. Raven was just happy he was laughing.

Carter smiled when Khalil danced into the kitchen, and Carter yucked when Blair greeted Khalil with a *'Hey lover.'*

He must've had a good sleep, Raven speculated, setting the dinner table.

"So, who wants to go first? Huddle? Actually-I'll go first," Khalil cut into his food. "Today, I witnessed an adoption at court. It was nice to see the new family and everyone happy."

Blair eyed Dad carefully. "And your low?"

"Well... . I've been thinking. You do a lot around here. I need to step it up more. So, I will." He looked at Blair closely. Both of their eyes were soft, and they held each other's gaze. Blair cleared her throat and looked away.

Carter cleared his throat next.

"Can I go?" he asked.

"Sure, baby," Blair sat up straighter in her chair.

"Ray helped me today. That was my high. I ain't got no lows, though," Carter spoke like he was waiting for someone to interrupt. No one did.

Raven's heart swelled as she felt flushed again. She hoped they couldn't see her cheeks turning red.

"We want you here." Raven nodded. Carter nodded back and took a drink of his juice.

Dinner continued with light conversation and a few laughs. It was music to Raven's starved ears.

"Have you ever taken out the trash?" Khalil asked Carter. Carter had started to help clear the dishes off the kitchen table.

"No."

"Like you've never carried it outside, you mean?" Khalil questioned. Carter shrugged his shoulders and shook his head again.

"Okay, well, it's simple. You lift the strings on the sides and pull the bag up out of the trashcan. Then sit it in the black bin outside. Okay?" Khalil instructed.

Khalil modeled it once for Carter. Raven watched her dad drop down into a semi-squat stance and pull the trash bag up out of the bin with one swift motion.

"You try." Khalil pointed to Carter.

Carter nodded his head and took over the bags from Khalil while they switched positions. Carter furrowed his eyebrows together as he attempted to hoist the bag out of the trashcan. His small muscles bulged from his arms, and he panted heavily. He grunted and lost his footing a bit — he steadied himself again and pulled the bag up once more. Carter lost his balance and stumbled back, still determined to get the sack out of the trashcan. The trashcan was obviously winning and too heavy for Carter. His arms shook as he pulled the bag up. Sweat formed at his hairline.

Raven and her parents stood back, letting their uncertainty take the lead. The sight of Carter as he struggled with the trashcan did something to Raven, and before long, she giggled. Then Blair. Then Khalil. Then surprisingly, Carter cracked a smile.

Carter sat the bag down, and it hit the floor with a loud smack. The family did something they had not done in a very long time. . . they shared a laugh. Deep belly laughs. The family snorted and gasped for breath. Blair had tears coming out of her eyes, and Khalil choked out a cough with his arm on the wall. His shoulders shook up and down as he snickered. The entire family roared with laughter at the sight of Carter sparring with the too heavy trash can.

Khalil took out his phone and FaceTimed Phoenix. He struggled to tell her through his laughs about Carter and the trash can. Raven heard them laughing together as Khalil helped Carter with the trash can.

Carter continued snickering, and Raven saw something she had never seen before in his eyes.

Hope.

We were going to make it, Raven decided.

CHAPTER 24

"Brown Girls, I got it!" Jasmine flashed a card in front of them at the lunch table. Raven looked at it carefully. Jasmine got her driver's license.

Jasmine was a year older than the rest of the girls, even though they were in the same grade. They knew she would be first to get her license, but Raven didn't think it was this soon. Their last few conversations flashed in Raven's mind. She didn't mention studying for a driver's test — it seemed out of the blue.

"How about a trip to NOLA after school today, ladies?" Jasmine danced. "I'm down," Trinity and Nia answered at the same time.

They turned to look at Raven.

"Okay." Raven felt the silent peer pressure.

"Wait — have you driven before? And whose car do you have?" Raven pressed.

"Girl, here you go. I have my brother's car. Ant has to work, and I told him I wanted to practice driving anyway, and he handed me the keys. He knows I have the car." Jasmine jingled her keys in front of Raven as Nia and Trinity squealed. Raven shook her head and said nothing else.

“Can I roll with y’all? I don’t have practice today,” Amir asked as he pulled up a chair at the table. His friends soon followed and pulled up chairs too.

“Of course! We out!” Jasmine clinked her keys once more. This was turning into a complete adventure.

The last bell rang, and Raven waited in front of the school for Jasmine.

“You ready, girl?” Jasmine was light on her feet, with her keys swinging in her hand. She had pep in her step. Trinity, Nia, and Amir came from another exit out of the school. Amir locked eyes with Raven and walked to her.

“You good?” He studied Raven’s face.

“Yeah, yeah, I’m okay,” She didn’t want to be a Nervous Nelly.

“So, what do you guys want to do first?” Jasmine asked as they piled into the car. Amir, Trinity, and Raven sat in the backseat. Nia climbed into the front while Jasmine fumbled with the radio.

“You said we were going to NOLA, right?” Amir asked.

“That’s fine with me. Ya’ll need to stop anywhere first?” Jasmine put on her sunglasses and peered at us from the rearview mirror. She put her foot on the gas, then removed it and placed her foot on the parking brake instead. She started the car.

"Let's swing by Wendy's first before we get on the highway," said Nia. Raven's stomach grumbled. She was a little hungry.

"Yeah, I could go for some nuggets," Raven admitted.

"Let's roll." Jasmine started the car, and her brother's loud engine roared to life. She checked her face in the rearview mirror. The windows were fogged from the car sitting all day. It was another unseasonably cool afternoon for November. Raven wore a hat over her curls.

"Put the defroster on," Amir instructed.

Jasmine crept out of the parking lot, slamming on her brakes, and they all flew forward in the car. Raven gasped at the jolt.

Jasmine fumbled with the controls, "Which one is the defroster?"

Amir reached from the back and turned the knob to defrost. Jasmine gave Amir a thumbs-up sign, and she turned the music back up. She tapped the brakes once more before giving it some gas. Trinity and Raven looked at each other.

Raven, Trinity, Nia, Jasmine, and Amir cruised. Raven rolled down her window from the back and felt a cool breeze on her face. The sun shone on her freckles and warmed her skin. Raven inhaled and closed her eyes. The sights, sounds, and smells of their little slice of Louisiana calmed her spirit.

Nia sat in the front seat dancing and moving to Pop Smoke on the radio. Jasmine had both hands on the steering wheel and was paying extra attention to the road. Trinity sat between Amir and Raven. Raven noticed the air blowing through Trinity's hair; it looked beautiful up against the swirling air. She looked like a movie star. Trinity had her eyes closed, and she bobbed her head to the music.

Nia turned the music up louder, and no one said a word; just vibed. No one had their phones out; they were in the moment.

Amir sat on the other side, and Raven looked at him as he looked at her. They held each other's gaze for a while before Trinity crossed her eyes at Raven, interrupting their trance. She burst out laughing.

Jasmine turned into the Wendy's parking lot and pulled into the drive thru. She pulled up to the ordering box and slammed on the brakes a third time that day. Jasmine needed to be first at everything, and she started firing off as soon as the car made a full stop.

"I need a number three, no cheese," said Jasmine.

Trinity sweetly cut in, *"Give me a large fry, no salt, please."*

Raven shouted from the back, *"I'll take a sweet tea, light ice."*

Amir asked, *"Is your ice cream machine working?"*

Jasmine spoke again, *"Umm, nevermind, forget that number three. Give me a number one, no tomato or pickle!"*

"I have a free French fry from my app, can you scan it?" Nia chimed in.

"Do you have any chocolate chip cookies?" Amir quizzed. He had a sweet tooth.

They shot questions into the ordering box with no mercy. Nia still had the music high, and they were yelling out the left side windows trying to get their order straight. Nia and Jasmine were going back and forth about using a coupon when it happened.

Raven heard a loud crunch, and the car made a lurching sound as it hurled forward. Everyone in the car flew forward and flopped all over the place as the car glided over something.

"Hello, hello? Is everything okay out there?" The voice from the box was filled with concern.

Raven gulped and tried to catch her breath.

Nia stared at Jasmine, whose face was red. She looked down in her lap, avoiding everyone's eyes.

Raven steadied herself to get a better look. Everyone seemed okay, just shaken up. She poked her head outside of the car.

Jasmine ran over the big, yellow stanchion pole in the drive-thru next to the ordering box. They ordered their food, and when Jasmine slipped her foot off the brake, she clipped a pole in the drive-thru window and took it down. Rode right over top of it. They sat tilted in the car.

Raven looked over at Amir as he held his mouth. Trinity breathed slowly and held back laughter. Nia could never hide her emotions and burst into a deep laugh with tears streaming from her face. Jasmine sat in the front seat, embarrassed. Cars beeped their horns all around them; they were sandwiched in, and no one could get around. They sat stuck overtop of a pole with the car leaning.

"Oh, shit!" Nia exclaimed.

"I knew it. I let her bully me right into a car accident. She done hit the Wendy's pole. We haven't even made it out of Lake Lacroix!" Raven cursed.

Amir glanced at Raven with shocked eyes and laughed even harder. She caught his gaze, and she, too — laughed. With heads thrown back, loud guffaws escaped their throats. Raven's eyes were crinkled at the corners, and she felt them pool with funny tears. She couldn't control noises that were escaping her, and she snorted and covered her mouth.

Amir's eyes widened as he attempted to slap her shoulder over Trinity's head. He couldn't reach since they sat tilted. This made the car even more hysterical, they finally realized they were sitting sideways in the Wendy's drive-thru stuck on a stanchion pole.

They giggled so hard they didn't hear police sirens in the distance. Lights flashed in the window, and Raven glanced to her left and spotted Khalil Jamison himself. She took a deep breath and rolled down the window again, this time not to order food — but to talk to her father.

CHAPTER 25

"You should've seen their asses sitting there overtop of a yellow pole. I was so embarrassed," Khalil said to Blair, Aunt Cocina, and Nana. They sat around the dinner table, and Khalil was giving his best performance, retelling the group how he found the kids in Wendy's drive thru.

"Babe, when I got there, and it's my baby! My baby! In the car stuck on a Wendy's pole. I'll never forgive you for this one, Ray." Khalil feigned hurt. Blair cackled with amusement. Even Carter found it funny.

"What were you guys thinking?" Nana had napkins at her eyes, wiping tears.

"I don't know! How was I supposed to know she wouldn't see the giant pole right next to the car? It's a big yellow pole. I don't know how she didn't see it."

They all hollered louder and held their stomachs. Even Carter had his hands over his mouth and tried not to laugh out loud.

Raven sat there with her arms folded, not finding anything funny.

"Lil, you know what that reminds me of? Remember that time I was trying to jump a fence, and I got stuck climbing over?"

Cocina turned to the rest of the table, "We were being chased by a dog, and Lil took the fence in one quick swoop! Over it, he went. That little fence took my ass out, and Lil had to come back for me. I had my bookbag on, and when I went over the fence, my bag got caught, and I just hung there like a limp rag." Aunt Cocina and Khail roared. So many memories between them.

"Your feet weren't even touching the ground. You were hanging off the fence screaming, 'Lil, Lil!!" Khalil chortled.

"And, where was I?" Nana's face was blank.

"You weren't home." Aunt Cocina took a sip of her water.

Nana looked away.

Khalil showed up to Wendy's and read Raven the riot act in front of her friends. He made Jasmine take a breathalyzer, and he had question after question. "*How did this happen? Were you guys drinking? Doing them drugs?"* He finally realized nothing shady had happened, and Jasmine accidentally slipped her foot off the brake and rode over the pole. Now he thought it was comedy night at the Jamison house. He stood up and balanced himself on one foot. "Babe, they were lopsided like this," he teetered around the table. "The cars were beeping around them screaming, '*damn kids!*'"

Cocina, Blair, and Khalil slapped the table, heads thrown back in cackles. Raven didn't think it was that funny. When

Khalil called Jasmine's dad and told him what happened, he came to the police station and picked up Jasmine. When leaving, her dad rode over the curb pulling out of the parking lot. The back tire smacked down on the road with a loud thud. Khalil sprinkled in that part of the story, too, whenever he told people about the "incident." Raven sat there quiet as they laughed at her. Parents had their way of ruining things.

Raven looked around and observed her family together. She realized this was the first time they ate dinner as a group. Aunt Cocina, Carter, and Nana. Aunt Cocina and Carter were permitted supervised visits through DCFS, and this was their third one. The first one was tense, Carter told Raven he didn't know what to expect.

Yes . . . he told her! Carter was finally talking. Not every day, and not all day. But here and there — he gave them glimpses.

Carter managed his anger by staying silent most days. But then again, he and Nana seemed to share a bond through yoga. He enjoyed the classes because there was no expectation to talk. Carter used a few of his first words at home to ask if they were going to yoga class again — until they went every Saturday. Carter enjoyed when his mom came over to visit, but he also enjoyed when she left to go home. He liked it even better when he got to stay on Sycamore Street. It brought him a sense of stillness, knowing that all the things and all the people supposed to be in the home — were.

God, he hoped they never needed him to say that out loud.

Cocina struggled to find words to explain grief to her son. She noticed he was less angry towards her. She was willing to meet him where he was and do whatever he wanted. She wanted to meet him on his terms and allow him to dictate the place, the time, and their interactions. All at the insistence of his therapist, Ms. Margaret. *"Let him lead. Let him decide when and how he wants to come back around to us,"* he overheard Ms. Margaret tell Aunt B.

And Carter did.

He called the shots and made the choices regarding the direction of his relationship with his mom. He unfurrowed his flowers. His layers peeled back. The caterpillar was emerging; the butterfly would be ready soon. It wasn't ready yet, but soon. Carter ruled the household, and he didn't even know it.

Carter watched Uncle Lil transform the past few weeks.

It was now December, and he had lived with them since August.

One thing Carter did and did well was laugh. He found Khalil hilarious. They were a family of jokesters, and where words were missing, laughs and giggles took over. When Khalil discovered Carter found him humorous, he changed and made more effort to make Carter laugh. He took him to football games, and he let Carter help him wax his car in the garage. That was huge — he let no one touch his car, but he let Carter help. He took it seriously, and he looked studious as he waxed and did what he could to please Khalil.

Khalil made it his business every day to check in with everyone in the house. He started at the top, *"Blair, do you need anything? Can I help with anything?"*

One day he came home from work early to surprise the family with dinner. He accidentally placed broccoli in the microwave for twenty minutes instead of two minutes to defrost. He fell asleep on the couch and woke up to the fire alarm screaming through the house, a smoking microwave, and broccoli on the verge of fire. Khalil didn't cook after that.

His mood extended to Raven. He asked about dance and school, and he genuinely listened. He didn't throw in any funny commentary to cut the mood. He tried to read between the lines and listen for things she didn't say. She just needed him home with them. That was all.

Huddle became an event these days. Khalil went first and always had some elaborate story about nothing.

It was nice.

It seemed like the house made a change. It wasn't a full one-eighty, but they were on their way. The rain clouds cleared from the Jamison home, and sunshine dared to peek through. They were ready.

CHAPTER 26

Raven walked through the hall on her way to Ms. Whitaker's office —slightly annoyed. Ms. Whitaker plucked her out from the lunchroom where prying eyes wanted to be in the know. She turned the corner towards Ms. Whitaker's office, and there sat Taylor.

This was a setup.

Raven turned to Ms. Whitaker and waited for her to explain her betrayal.

"Now, Ms. Raven, please take a seat so we can talk."

Raven continued to stand.

"Please — sit down, it's okay." Ms. Whitaker pointed to Raven's favorite beanbag. She sat down across from Taylor.

"Taylor has requested a mediation between you and her."

"She did?"

"Yes, she did," Ms. Whitaker repeated.

Taylor sat quietly.

"Taylor," Ms. Whitaker began.

"Look, Raven, I don't want no problems." Taylor rolled her neck right away.

"I don't either."

"Is there something that you feel Raven has done to you?" Ms. Whitaker turned toward Taylor.

"Yes. I know last year she tried to date Justin . . . and she talked about my dad."

Back to the Dad thing. Raven sighed. She couldn't hide her disdain. "I did not, Taylor. I don't know what else to say. I apologize for that. If you feel it was intentional, it was not."

Raven explained the IG post to Ms. Whitaker. Raven even mentioned Taylor and her family recently coming to Raven's house for dinner. "And I don't know where you got this story about me trying to date Justin. You two are perfect for each other." Raven crossed her arms.

"See! You see!" Taylor's voice rose, and she pointed her finger at Raven. "This is exactly what I mean."

Ms. Whitaker gave Raven a strange look. Raven tried calming herself. She looked around the room and counted....

She started again. "You know what — you're right. That wasn't cool. I have never tried to date, Justin. Ever. But I believe you're just throwing things up to see what will stick."

"Taylor, do you believe it was intentional? Sometimes our perceptions of the situation can be skewed by-well, anything really. If you really believe that it was intentional, then we'll sit here all day hashing this out. Just like we talk in our sessions," Ms. Whitaker nodded.

In our sessions? They had sessions? Raven perked up.

Taylor sat quietly with her hands in her lap. A tear fell from her eye. “You know, I look at you, and I remember when my parents were happy. I remember when my mom would come home and greet my dad with so much love in her face. You complain and worry. You play the victim. You have dance, and you’ve had dance for years. You take it all for granted.”

Raven was stunned. For the second time in two weeks, someone told her she played the victim. “Taylor, I’ve been trying to figure you out for years. I never thought you liked me, and I never understood why. There never seemed to be reason.”

“I just gave you reasons,” Taylor’s voice still raised.

“I hear you, I’m just saying I never had reasons before. You sprung this on me, and I’m trying to figure it all out. But I don’t think I play the victim,” she countered. Jasmine could say that to her, but she wasn’t about to let Taylor say it too — not without her defending herself.

“And Raven? What are your issues with Taylor?” Ms. Whitaker asked.

Raven sat and thought. She went through different situations in her head. An eye roll and finger snap. A whisper directed towards her. Raven remembered the confusion she felt at some of those behaviors. When she tried to piece together a story, nothing seemed to fit. She couldn’t pinpoint a time when Taylor directly did anything to her. She wondered what it was they were really arguing about all these years.

“I got nothing,” Raven shrugged.

“I knew you wouldn’t take it seriously,” Taylor’s leg shook up and down.

“Now is your time, Raven. What’s on your mind?” Ms. Whitaker pressed.

“I thought about what you just said. About perception. There have been times when I thought Taylor was talking about me and when she rolled her eyes at me. There've been times when I thought a lot of things, but I never knew for sure. Maybe my perception was off. I don’t know; I just look at things so differently right now. If you came to me a month ago and we had this conversation, then I probably would’ve had an answer. But now — I don’t know, it just doesn’t seem like something I want to keep focusing on.”

She looked directly at Taylor.

“I’m sorry, Taylor, I’m really sorry if I have ever offended you, I apologize because that was never my intention. If you think I rolled my eyes at you, or you thought I wanted to talk to Justin, all of those things; whatever, I’m sorry. Especially about the Justin thing, because that’s a bald-faced lie. But I can’t sit here and point to things you’ve done to me because I really don’t know. If you want to move forward from here — we can. If not, that's fine too. But I don't want to go tit-for-tat about what we both did or didn't do. We've been at this for years, and really, for what?"

Ms. Whitaker looked between Raven and Taylor like she was at a tennis match. She said nothing. She sat there silently, supporting both of her students. Taylor made sure no more tears fell from her face. She dabbed them before that could happen again. Her back straightened, and her face hardened.

Maybe Raven had been wrong about this moment. Her speech had been her waving the white flag and extending an olive branch. But the way Taylor was looking at her, it seemed as if to Taylor — Raven may have declared war.

"I'm done," Taylor mumbled.

The bell rang, and she gathered her things. Taylor left Ms. Whitaker's office first and didn't look over her shoulder.

CHAPTER 27

"Look at this shit right here," Trinity whispered. Her voice was laced with disgust. Had it not been for Raven's churning stomach, she probably would have said the same thing. Her body was on fire. She felt the heat coursing through her chest. Taylor was auditioning for Raven's captain position on the dance team.

"*The bylaws state she only has one routine before the team votes."* Ms. Adams reminded everyone.

Humph, one dance was too much if you asked Raven. They would have to revisit those bylaws. She watched on in anger. As sweat dripped from Taylor's head, she hit every move with her trademark half-smirk, half-smile. Her moves were poised and polished. Taylor was good — incredibly good. Raven would give her that. She wanted her to beat her ass; Raven could feel it in her bones. Raven knew she brought this on herself. When she carpeted Taylor, she knew there would be blowback — but she didn't expect this.

A few weeks earlier, after the incident, Nia confronted Raven about her behavior with Taylor. Nia used words like *"immature"* and *"instigator."* Raven tried to argue with Nia, but she shut it down and wouldn't let her get a word in. Nia ended with "Do better!" and walked away. Like she was exasperated or something.

Raven turned and looked at Nia, wondering who she believed was being immature and an instigator now.

"Anndd thank you for that piece, Taylor." Ms. Adams blew her whistle, interrupting Raven's thoughts.

"Ms. Raven, you're uppp," she sang. "Now — as the standing team captain, you get one extra minute for your piece. Let's get it done."

Taylor had challenged Raven. She requested to settle their dispute on the floor mat. For Raven's spot. An official challenge hadn't happened in over five years, Raven checked with Ms. Adams for that information. You would have to send a request to the physical education department and have it signed by the vice principal. Taylor went through all the proper channels to confront Raven, and here they stood. She meant business. Raven stretched and looked over at Nia.

"You got this," Nia mouthed with a nod. She always had Raven's back.

Taylor finished her piece, and Raven got up to go next, on the defense. The gym seemed completely quiet today. Normally the ancient air conditioner would sound deafening, but today it was eerily quiet. Even it came to listen to the battle. Raven surveyed the scene while she counted. She inhaled slowly five times and exhaled slower. She looked for five things she saw, then four, then three....

"Calm your body first. You are exactly where you need to be . . ." Nana's voice echoed in Raven's mind.

The music began, and Raven started slow. She could feel the drums deep in her chest. She remembered the drums from their day at the docks. The way the women watched Raven brought a smile to her face. She would smile later, right now, she had a challenge to win.

Raven's body swayed and gyrated to the beat with her arms spread out to the sky. Raven dropped onto the mat and rolled her body with precision and grace.

Make it look effortless, Raven willed.

She didn't see anyone and heard nothing. She let the music guide her to a faraway place. The instrumental beats whispered a song only Raven could hear, and she heard it well. Raven changed the tempo of the music and fell into a jazz routine, but baby — Raven gave them hip hop, mixed with jazz, and sprinkled some ballet in there too. The bass intensified, and she switched into Chris Brown's "Go Crazy Challenge." For four minutes, Raven gave them all of her. Just a brown girl from Lake Lacroix, Louisiana, who liked to dance.

Raven let her anger and feelings speak for her. She left the words at home and let her body do the talking today. She couldn't fix her family, couldn't fix Carter, and couldn't fix Taylor.

But in that moment, Raven knew that she could fix herself, just by being who she was — and that was enough.

Today, Raven kicked ass. She felt it, and she knew it. The doubt erased from her mind. People would love her for who she was. She was safe. It was not her responsibility to fix everyone and everything. She would build the life she wanted to live and would do it with her head held high, ready for it all.

She finished her routine with tears in her eyes. There were so many things she questioned, but dancing; this was one thing she was sure about. Raven's chest heaved up and down as she struggled to catch her breath. When she came to, the room erupted in claps and cheering. Raven blinked away salty tears. She eyed Taylor, standing off to the side with her arms folded.

She got the right one today, Raven scoffed.

She didn't come to lose. The once empty gym was filled with people who watched the battle. Raven saw Amir, Trinity, and Jasmine in the crowd, all of them cheering and smiling. Trinity finally sat down. She had been standing next to the mat since she first saw Taylor walk in.

"All right, all right, all right." Ms. Adams blew her whistle. "Now, as coach, I have to say that challenges keep us strong. They don't happen too often, but they are there for a reason. They strengthen us as a team and individuals. They help us see errors. Always look for your role and how you can become better when someone challenges you. Sometimes you get what you thought you wanted, and other times it forces your hand. Always find the lesson." Raven thought Ms. Adams was talking to her.

With a clap of her hands, Ms. Adams finished. "Okkk! Voting time! Hands in the air for Taylor?" Jessica raised her hand along with a few others. Raven sucked her teeth.

"Okay, hands in the air for Raven."

One by one, everyone else on the team raised their hand to support Raven. Nia raised both hands. Even the people who came into the gym to watch raised their hand for her. For her! Raven unclenched her hands and relaxed her shoulders.

"It looks like Ms. Raven has defended her position." Ms. Adams nodded as the room cheered.

Raven looked at Taylor as she walked off. Taylor swung around and glanced back. Raven was sorry a misunderstanding started this year's long cold war between them. It saddened Raven they weren't able to mend their differences. She accepted the fact that she and Taylor probably would never be friends. Cordial — but never friends. Raven had to be okay with not being liked or being friends with everyone, and that included Taylor. She didn't want to be cordial anyway, that was clear. And that was okay; it had to be. There would be no happy ending, there would be no friendship.

They were two young, brown girls agreeing to walk away. There would be no beef. It was settled right here on the dance mat, anyway.

Taylor walked off in a huff with Jessica. Amir, Jasmine, Nia, and Trinity surrounded Raven. Everyone danced and laughed, imitating some of Raven's moves. Raven knew who her family was. It was the family Raven had created. Right here, this was her support system. She so depended on their friendship and let it cover her like a shield. She realized she didn't need to depend on them because they were always there supporting her anyway. It was time for Raven to rise, like a phoenix.

CHAPTER 28

"I really need a fill." Raven examined her nails as she rode home that Wednesday afternoon. The bus slowed to a stop in front of The Hill. When she had to fight Carter off like a grown man weeks ago, her nails had pinged off one by one like in a cartoon.

No one would be home. Khalil was working overtime, and Blair was running errands. Carter was on a scheduled visit with his mentor. She was alone for a few hours and didn't know what to do.

"Do you have a lot of homework?" Nia asked, walking home.

"No, not too much. I think I'm going to get my nails done. Wanna roll?" "No, I gotta watch Bryce tonight. My mom has to do something with Ms. Twizz."

"Ok, well, I'll call you later then." Raven waved goodbye as she turned around down the Hill in the opposite direction. Raven ran in the house and changed her clothes. She was going to ride her bike down to the nail salon, the shop wasn't too far from home. Raven zipped her jacket up to her neck.

The weather was changing, and it was getting brisk. Raven still couldn't believe the chill that had settled over Lake Lacroix. People commented that it had been the coolest fall in years. There still hung a lingering sweet smell of honeysuckle, and no matter how much the cold crept in, that scent was there every day, making its presence known. Raven woke up a few days before, and there was a light fog hanging over Lake Lacroix. It was beautiful to see it so still and serene.

"Gotta watch people when it's cooler outside. They take all they secrets inside with them," Ms. Twizz said one day on the bus. She attributed a lot of things to the weather, Raven chuckled.

She grabbed her bike and continued her route down Sycamore Street. They had lived on Sycamore Street her entire life. She gazed at the oak trees wrapped around the street that seemed to line the skies. The wind whipped past her face, and it made her eyes burn and then tear. She peered at the children who rode their bikes, walked down the street, and played tag. Raven noticed the older generations, most of them sitting on their porches and in their chairs, people watching. Raven couldn't help but think: as the weather changed, what secrets would they bring inside? What secrets had the Jamison's brought inside?

Raven entered Lake Lacroix's Nail Salon and signed in. She sat down and took out her phone to check her IG.

"Ray?"

Raven glanced up and saw Aunt CoCo looming in front of her, holding a container full of nail polish. She was wearing a

Lake Lacroix Nail Shop vest. Her hair was pulled up in a tight ponytail, her edges were screaming to be let free. It was the ponytail you knew was ugly, but it was the best you could do in a pinch; it was acceptable for a day at work. Cocina's eyebrows were clearly drawn on, and in her nose sat a small stud nose piercing. The fact Aunt Cocina would walk out the house looking like that told Raven her aunt was serious this time.

Aunt Cocina startled Raven. She forgot just how much Aunt Cocina looked like her father, and any other day she would have found the situation funny, but today she didn't laugh.

"I didn't know you worked here, Aunt CoCo," she glanced up from her seat.

"I just started; it's only been about a week. I didn't know you were coming. Did you have an appointment?"

"No, no, I didn't have an appointment — I normally just walk in. This is my first time seeing you here," Raven looked around.

"Well, if you're free, I can do your nails next," Cocina offered.

"I'd like that."

Raven followed Aunt Cocina over to her workstation, where Cocina was prepped and ready to go. All her stuff was neatly lined up and labeled at her small desk. Her gloves were laid on her mat along with clean towels, hand soaps, lotions, emery boards, and nail polish. Raven was impressed at the setup. Cocina had everything she needed, and she sat down and got right to work.

"So, what would you like to get today, Miss Ray?"

"I guess we can just do a pink gel polish," she shrugged.

"Gel? You should really let me try some dip powder on you. I think you'd like it better." Cocina held up Raven's hands and inspected her nails.

"You know what, I've heard of that — but I don't know. I like what I like."

"Okay, well, if you change your mind, let me know."

This entire conversation was so awkward Raven didn't know where to begin. It felt fake, but this was the most conversation she had with her aunt in a while. They had visited Aunt Cocina when she was away in her program, but Raven had the protection of her mom and Nana. Not that she needed protection from Aunt Cocina, but she could take the backseat when Nana and Mom were around. She didn't have to think; they did it for her. Raven pressed forward.

"So how you been Aunt CoCo?" she asked her directly.

It was bold of Raven. Cocina knew it too.

"I-I am okay," Cocina focused on Raven's nails.

Just as she had read Taylor's honesty, she read Aunt CoCo's too.

"This time is different. It must be. At some point, I have to change the narrative. It has to start with me," Cocina mulled. Raven listened to her aunt's words. They sounded like bullshit to her. Raven's dad wasn't always right, but he also wasn't always wrong. He was correct about one thing. Carter had been through the wringer, and they were the ones left to deal with it.

"What happened that night? The night they took him?" Raven questioned.

Cocina swallowed.

"They wouldn't even let me get his clothes. We were sitting. We were talking. He was telling me about some project he had to do at school. He was making a Solar System and needed Styrofoam balls to make the planets. His project was due the next day, and he told me about it for weeks. I was too. . . loaded to remember. I put on my coat and was going to run to Walgreens and take the stuff he needed. When I opened the door, Ms. Cottman's funky ass was standing there with two police officers. For a second, my heart dropped. I prayed that it wasn't Khalil. It wasn't him. Ms. Cottman threw some paperwork my way. I had already talked to your mom earlier that day and asked if she would take in Carter. I tried to tell that to Ms. Cottman, but she wasn't trying to hear it."

"And Carter?" Raven leaned in.

“He clung to my leg . . he said he couldn’t go through this again.”

Raven pushed slightly away from her aunt’s workstation and put some distance between them. Her chair rolled back and almost hit someone walking by.

“Excuse me,” she said to them. *He couldn’t go through this again. She didn’t even know Carter was in foster care before.* She wondered if her dad knew. There were so many things they didn’t tell each other, and apparently, Cocina was in the don’t-say-nothing-club too. She wasn’t sure what to say to her aunt after that admission; she changed the subject.

“And I think you should talk to Nana. Really talk. You and her are in the same room, but you talk past each other. Around each other. It’s weird, and we notice,” Raven admitted.

Cocina remained quiet.

“You should come to one of her yoga classes with us. Carter really likes them,” she suggested.

Her face reddened again.

She wondered if she had said too much. Cocina remained quiet for what seemed like an eternity before speaking.

“You know, when I started doing the work like really started doing the work and not bullshitting, I realized just how much damage I have done to Carter. And I didn’t even know any better. I didn’t understand because I have been so used to dysfunction and so prepared to accept it as normal life. This was our lot in life as women, as Black women: we suffer, we bear it all, and they take it all. You make a way, and you figure it out. Guess what that is? Trauma! I'm preparing myself to accept the trauma. That's what I thought I deserved." She shook her head.

Tears welled up in Raven's eyes all the time these days, and today was no different. Raven struggled to wipe her face with Aunt Cocina holding her hands, picking at her nails. She furrowed her chin into her arm, trying to catch her falling tears. Aunt CoCo grabbed a tissue and dabbed Raven's face for her. Raven didn't know what she was expecting, but not what Aunt Cocina said. Aunt Cocina was so quiet at the house, at least when Khalil was there. But when she was alone, her aunt could be strong and well-spoken. She, too — was a survivor.

Raven still got to see bits and pieces of her personality when Cocina and her mom sat at the house, having a girl talk. They would laugh and whisper. Raven would hear her Mom say, *'Girl, you heard about Rahshana an'em?"* And they would just laugh and laugh. Those were the times when Raven got to see Aunt CoCo's personality. So, hearing the person talking now sounded like someone totally different. *More word vomit.* Raven thought to herself.

“Carter-Carter has been. Having a hard time.” Raven didn’t know how else to put it, so she said it the way it came out.

Aunt CoCo buffed Raven’s index finger harder.

” What do you mean?”

“He has trouble sleeping, eating. He hides food, and he’s fighting everyone at school. But the thing that scares me the most is he doesn’t really talk. It’s gotten better, a lot better, actually. But still. I worry about him all the time. We are all trying, but we don’t know what to do.”

Aunt CoCo buffed Raven’s finger harder and faster. Cocina’s supervisor stood over her shoulder and watched. Coco sensed someone standing behind her; her shoulders relaxed, and she slowed down.

“Okay. . . okay,” she repeated.

Cocina and Raven were quiet. Raven listened to the sounds of the surrounding shop. The way the other patrons peered over at Cocina and Raven let her know they were listening to their conversation. Aunt CoCo lowered her voice.

“That’s why this time has to be different. It will be different. He’s older, he’s already seen too much and heard too much. Had to worry about things a little boy should never have to worry about. Those are wrongs I can never right, but I’m here now. I’m here now. I am showing up, and I am doing the work. Now go wash your hands.”

She pointed Raven to the sink and banged the emery board onto the table. Raven stood up and finally took a breath. She didn't realize she held it in during their talk. She washed her hands and returned to Aunt Cocina's workstation, where she had the polish out and ready.

"Give him some time." Aunt Cocina picked up right where she left off. "He'll come around. And don't take the food from his room. Leave it there until he's ready. I know that's gonna be hard for your mom."

They both nodded their heads in agreement.

"He doesn't like for people to ask him direct questions, but he will respond when asked. Just give him some time, he'll come around," she said. CoCo began rubbing lotion on to Raven's hands and massaging them.

"Thank you, Ray. Thank you for being his big cousin. He's never had a big cousin, it's just you."

Raven thought for a second. CoCo was right, she was Carter's only cousin. A thought flashed across her mind, and she giggled.

"Remember a few years ago when you came over, and you told dad you paid all your bills with 'nature's credit card?'"

Aunt Cocina's shoulders rose up and down as a deep laugh escaped from her belly. Raven locked eyes with her aunt and giggled.

"Your dad didn't find it so funny," Cocina wiped funny tears from her eyes. She was right. Raven recounted her dad's face changing and his eyes hardening. Nothing related to Aunt Cocina was amusing, at least not to him. "He's coming around," she lamented, "Give him some time." Raven used Aunt Cocina's words.

"And you, baby girl — are all done. Tell me what you think," Aunt Coco looked down nervously.

Raven examined her nails, each of them crafted with love and care, the exact colors, and sizes that she wanted. Cocina even added an extra diamond on her pinky fingers. Aunt CoCo really outdid herself today. She had a talent.

"They're beautiful." she breathed. "Thank you so much, Aunt CoCo." Aunt CoCo beamed. Raven only brought $35 with her to pay for her manicure, and the bill came to $25. She rummaged through her purse anyway looking for the credit card Blair let her keep for emergencies only. She needed to pay Aunt CoCo more than $35. She needed her aunt to know her worth. Raven thought this was an emergency and the perfect time to use the card.

CHAPTER 29

Raven was halfway to gym class when Ms. Whitaker caught up with her in the hallway.

"Ms. Raven, hey you!" She exclaimed. "Got some time to come talk to me?"

"Sure," Raven turned in the corridor and walked toward her office. Raven and Ms. Whitaker's lighthearted groups morphed into more and more frequent individual sessions. Raven knew Blair had intervened and plotted again with Ms. Whitaker. Every time Raven relaxed into Ms. Whitaker's beanbag chairs, the floodgates opened, and the words spilled from her. Ms. Whitaker sat there, staring back. She nodded her head and snapped her fingers when the conversation called for it. Raven knew she was listening, and sometimes that was enough.

"Raven, I thought we could play Jenga today. Have you played before?" "Yes, that's fine."

"Great, set it up, and let's get started." Ms. Whitaker took a drink from her large water bottle filled with all kinds of juices and berries. Raven did as she was told and began inspecting the cards. They were a colorful deck of cards with corresponding Jenga pieces, and each card had a question. Therapy Jenga. They were playing Therapy Jenga.

"I'll go first," Ms. Whitaker offered.

Good. Raven wasn't in the mood to lead this thing off.

Ms. Whitaker pulled a green block from the tower and plucked a green card. She read from the card, "What is something you have a hard time telling people about yourself?" Ms. Whitaker blushed. It was so brief Raven almost missed it had she not been paying attention. "Well, I would say I'm just like you guys. I come from where you come from, and some things you guys have experienced I've been through. I see myself in my students, and I try to be what I needed at your age."

Raven was unsure of what to do. She felt her own cheeks getting red. Ms. Whitaker's words felt genuine. She looked around the room again, noticing Black and brown faces still on the walls, now doubled. Ms. Whitaker had added more pictures and faces, more melanin. She glanced at Raven over her glasses, waiting for Raven to break the silence.

"My turn." Raven pulled a red block and pulled a red card. "When was the last time you stood up for yourself?" Raven read aloud. A lump formed in her throat. When was the last time she stood up for herself? Did she let anyone walk all over her? She wasn't sure, it wasn't something she regularly thought about.

"I don't think I've stood up for myself lately. I haven't had reasons to." Raven twirled a curl around her finger and glanced at the clock.

"I would have to disagree," Ms. Whitaker retorted.

"Why?"

"A little birdie told me Taylor French challenged your spot on the dance team. You marched in there and defended your position." Ms. Whitaker shrugged her shoulders and rolled her eyes.

"Yes, I did!"

"Well, don't you think that's standing up for yourself?"

"No, no, I don't." *But why didn't I?* Raven thought. *Why didn't I see that as me standing up for myself?*

"You know what I see? I see a girl ready to take what she wants —whatever that may be. Only you can figure it out," Ms. Whitaker nodded.

"I felt like I needed to stand up for myself with you," Raven admitted.

"Oh? In what way?"

"I saw your notebook last year. You wrote *'Raven Jamison, poor self-expression."* She repeated. She tried to say it in Ms. Whitaker's voice.

Ms. Whitaker was quiet.

Raven couldn't read her reaction, but she knew she was being unfair. She should not have brought that up. But oh well.

Apologize, Raven thought, *your issue isn't with Ms. Whitaker.*

Ms. Whitaker shifted in her seat.

"You know what, tell me then. Tell me who you are. Do you think you express yourself? Do you think you hide yourself?" She sat straight up in her chair, facing Raven.

Raven mulled for what seemed like forever. The room was thick with tension. The heater purred from the corner of the room. It was mostly quiet, but today its hum was louder than ever.

"I hide behind my friends. I let them take the lead. I express myself sometimes as part of a group. Never alone." Raven conceded. This was now the third time someone accused Raven on hiding behind her friends. One thing she knew; where there is smoke, there's fire. The thought vexed her.

Ms. Whitaker's eyes softened.

"What do you think can be done to *'see'* yourself?"

"Dancing . . . I'll let dance do the talking for me right now." Raven entertained the idea of where dance could take her, and she found more pros than cons.

When Taylor challenged Raven, not only did it make her burst with confidence, but Taylor's audacity also peeved her. It was time for Raven to use her wings and soar above the pack. There were so many things that made her nervous, but she knew for sure dance was hers. She had her "thing" all along.

"I think that's an impressive start. You're a beautiful brown girl. And I'm sorry you had to read that on my desk but look at it this way. You've proven me wrong. Your self-expression has changed so much. I think you see it now too." Ms. Whitaker said with a wink. The bell rang, and a few seconds later, Raven left Ms. Whitaker's office. She didn't need to count or calm herself. She was okay.

CHAPTER 30

The Jamison family silently sparred in the living room. Khalil sat across from Cocina. Raven sat facing Blair, Phoenix, and Carter, who shared a loveseat. Ms. Margaret settled on the other side of the room, facilitating the meeting. They prepared for the family session and knew it was upcoming, but it still worried the entire family. Blair spent the day cleaning like a maniac. She bleached and scrubbed the countertops squeaky clean. Raven walked in from school and choked from all the chemicals. Carter was his usual quiet self, but he seemed . . . extra fidgety. He was walking around touching random things in the house, and Raven swore she saw him counting the paint splatters on their popcorn ceiling in the hallway. Khalil arrived home early, went into his bedroom, and took a nap. Her dad was not the napping type. This concerned her.

“Okay, team,” Ms. Margaret turned towards everyone. “Let’s get started. For those of you who are not familiar with me, I’m Margaret Brewster, Carter’s therapist for the past few months since he’s been in transition. I’ve also been working closely with Blair, and she understood that for the team to best support Carter, we have to come together for him.”

Everyone locked eyes around the room. Carter’s team. Our family.

"Let's start with an activity." Ms. Margaret walked around the room with a small basket. "I put everyone's name in this basket, I'm going to shake it, and you guys pull one name. Don't say whose name you pulled just yet. I want you to think about the person and what you admire about them. We'll then share out with the group."

Someone inhaled sharply, Raven couldn't tell who. The family quietly did as they were told. The basket went around slowly like they were hoping for a golden ticket. Raven pulled a name out of the basket, and her heart skipped a beat. Phoenix. She had Nana. Eyes were flying around the room with no words spoken. She saw Nana lean over Carter's shoulder to see whose name he pulled. She giggled.

"Raven, would you like to start?" Ms. Margaret said.

No. No, I don't, Raven scowled. Of course, Ms. Margaret would pick her first. She exhaled. "She's nice" —

"Hold up," Ms. Margaret rose to her feet. "Turn towards whoever you have and look them in their eyes. Remember, you want them to know how you feel, but they also need you to use your entire body speaking to them. So, give *'her'* your full attention. Face her and look her in the eyes as you speak."

Raven turned towards Nana and sighed. She started again. "Nana, you are fun. You keep us laughing, and you are easy to talk to. You just 'know' things. I love your style and especially like your yoga class. I can tell that it makes you happy too."

Nana sat quietly searching the walls. Her eyes were wet already, but she refused to let them spill over. She nodded her head. Nana didn't have words for Raven just yet.

Ms. Margaret nodded her head,

"Blair — your turn."

Blair twisted her body, facing Cocina.

"Cocina . . . what I've always admired about you is you do your own thing. You don't care what anyone thinks. You've always beaten your own drum and been your own person. And you make us laugh. I miss our girl talks."

Cocina shook her head and blinked back tears threatening to spill. Raven saw so much of Nana inside of Cocina. In her eyes, in her body movements. The way she tried so hard to compel herself not to cry, not to break down. Raven thought that's exactly what they both needed. A good cry.

Khalil got up and walked into the kitchen, and Raven heard the refrigerator door open. Khalil grabbed a few bottles of water and returned to the room and passed them around. Khalil's snickers turned into full laughter. He interrupted and said — "CoCo, you remember that time we lived on Monstera Road, and you convinced the electric company to pay the bill in oranges?" Khalil leaned against the dining room wall and took sips from his water bottle. "Mom had been gone for a few days. The electric company came to the house to turn off the electric, and we only had a crate of oranges we picked the day before. CoCo convinced the electric company to keep our electric on in exchange for the crate of oranges. These fools agreed and left with fruit, and we got to keep the lights on another night."

The room fell out in laughter. One thing about their family, they would laugh. Cocina and Khalil slapped each other's arms, snickering.

"It was all we had at the time," Cocina struggled to catch her breath. She was holding her sides, amused.

"I didn't know that." Nana's voice was soft, and she wasn't laughing. The room fell hush, and eyes turned to Phoenix.

"Ms. Phoenix, how does that make you feel hearing that?" Ms. Margaret leaned in.

"It's a damn slap in the face. I did my best. I didn't have much help, and Courtney did what he did. I thought we were past this shit. I'm just saying, I didn't know this happened." Phoenix shifted in her seat.

The room fell quiet again as Ms. Margaret softly spoke.

"We have to forgive ourselves for things we did when we didn't know any better. You did what you thought was best at the time, just like we're all doing what we think is best right now. You've grown and changed, and so has everyone else. We have to learn to give each other more grace. Whenever I get upset about something someone did to me, I ask myself, *'do I want to preserve this relationship? Or do I want to walk away from this person completely?'* If the answer is to preserve the relationship, then we have to show each other more grace and patience. We have to be slower to anger and quicker to listen and understand. Some of our relationships can be mended, just by better communication."

Phoenix sat back in her chair, uncrossing her arms.

"Nice work, guys. . . Cocina?" Ms. Margaret moved on.

The room hushed and turned toward Cocina. Raven glanced at Nana and gave her a weak smile. Nana nodded her head and sniffled.

Cocina breathed and started. "Khalil . . . Lil. He . . . you. . . you were my protector. You saved me in so many ways. I was a terrible kid," she chuckled. The room quieted again as everyone sat with bated breath.

"I remember when I first got my cycle. I was so scared, wondering what happened. Lil bought me pads. He walked to the corner store in a snowstorm for me that day. I remember because he came back and said — *'I don't know how to use these things, so you're on your own.'"* Cocina giggled. "Do you remember that?" She turned to Khalil.

He nodded his head, and Raven saw a twinkle in his eye as they reminisced.

"Lil is my superhero. My Cop." Khalil and Cocina caught each other's eyes and held them. Cocina's brimmed with tears that she hastily wiped away, hoping no one saw. Everyone saw — and they all had the same tears.

Khalil sat in a trance, watching his baby sister. His hands gripping the couch, wanting to run to her, but he resisted. "You have her eyes," he said blankly. Khalil looked between Cocina and his mom. He saw so many similarities. Not realizing, he had those same similarities. Jamison eyes.

"I've failed you, CoCo. I've failed you." Khalil sobbed. His shoulder's shuddered back, and his body trembled.

"No-no, you didn't, Lil. Don't do that. You were a teenager, what were you supposed to do? You had to survive. We survived. We survived." Cocina wept. Raven's heart ached at her dad's admission. She had never seen him cry — ever. He was always larger than life. She wanted to run to her dad and throw her arms around him. Khalil walked over to where Cocina was sitting, and he grabbed her hand. He helped her to her feet, and they stood face to face. The air was heavy with truth. Brother and sister mourned together. Cocina and Khalil embraced while the others looked on. There wasn't a dry eye in the room. Ms.

Margaret didn't interrupt the moment, she let it linger and allowed them to have their time together.

After a few minutes, she said, "Good work guys, let's continue. . . Khalil, you want to go?"

He took a deep breath and cleared his throat. "Carter. . . you've changed me in a lot of ways. You make me remember being a kid. We want you here. You've completed our circle, and for that, I am grateful."

Phoenix shifted in her seat, paying attention to Khalil's words. Carter gazed around the room, avoiding eyes. His hands were clenched, and he sat straight in his chair — perched, ready for anything. Carter wondered if maybe, just maybe, he didn't have to be. He examined everyone in the room, all there for him. He un-crinkled his eyebrows and relaxed his body.

"Thank you," he whispered.

"Nice guys. You sound beautiful right now," Miss Margaret's eyes shone. "Phoenix?"

"Okay, y'all," Phoenix sat up in her chair and snapped her fingers. "Blair, you bust your ass for your family. I see you running around here paying special attention to everyone. You are the glue. With all sincerity, you are my spirit animal. You are the mom I wished I knew how to be when I needed to be her." Although Phoenix was speaking to Blair, her eyes fixated on her children, Khalil and Cocina. "And I don't mean to take this thing over, but Lil

. . . I am forever grateful for the man you've become despite the things I didn't teach you. I don't say it much because I try not to dwell in that energy... but somewhere along the process, I stopped listening to both of you. I did what I thought was best for me . . . for us . . ." her voice trailed off. "Your dad. . . at least he never stole no money, and he never raped you guys. I know the feeling of seeing your abuser every day. I thought, '*Shit, everything else I can manage.'* Me and the kids, I can manage. Everything that I went through — I thought we went through it together." Phoenix expressed herself passionately, and some of what she said, Raven had heard before while visiting Aunt Cocina in her program. Other admissions she heard for the first time. Nana spoke quickly as if she was afraid someone may interrupt her. She sighed. This time her body settled into the couch in defeat.

"Phoenix, please don't shut down. Talk to us. What's on your mind?" Ms. Margaret asked.

"I just see things differently, that's all."

"How do you see it?" Bair sat up.

"I just. . . we. I grew up with my children. That's all," Phoenix lamented.

Phoenix's words hung in the air. Khalil and Cocina's legs both shuddered nervously. Carter and Raven were biting their nails, and Blair dabbed at her eyes. Cocina leapt up from the couch over Phoenix and pointed a finger in her face.

"And what about me being in foster care? Did we go through that together too?" Cocina demanded. Phoenix winced. The memories physically pained her.

Raven looked at Ms. Margaret, waiting for her to stop this train wreck. She didn't at first. "Remember, watch the way we talk to each other. These are relationships that we want to save, but also we need to be open to hearing each other's truth." Ms. Margaret didn't rise from her seat, and the tension in the room was thick. She wondered if she should open a window for some air.

Cocina sat back down and shook her leg feverishly.

"Phoenix, what do you hear Cocina saying?" Ms. Margaret asked.

"I was a terrible mom, and all her issues are my fault."

"That's one assessment. Khalil? What do you hear right now?"

Khalil communicated directly to Phoenix. "You weren't a terrible Mom. Actually, hearing your reasoning for staying, now it makes more sense to me. I think a lot of our issues started when you began drinking. That's when things got really bad."

That part was true, Phoenix admitted. That time in her life was a little hazy. Nights when the children had to fend for themselves for dinner, and weekends when they put her to bed. There were times the children were left to wonder where

Phoenix was and if she was safe. Or was she worried about them like they were about her? She fussed with them for taking away her liquor when she had never been a big drinker in the first place. It was Courtney who always had his lips wrapped around a bottle of something. Once he passed away, all that changed, and Phoenix picked up where he left off.

As Phoenix's alcohol addiction deepened, her disconnection from her children grew and grew. With one bitter sip after another, she let the bottle take her away to another place. She didn't have to think about the lonely late nights or having to raise a daughter on her own. She didn't even know how. She never had a good relationship with Elise. The same way Elise had been tough and cold with her, she was with Cocina.

Then one day, CPS showed up. They said Cocina's school had alleged neglect. She had not attended school in over three weeks. The school called a few times, and Phoenix was not home. Cocina finally admitted to school she had not seen her mom in a few weeks. Khalil was already away at college by then. Phoenix let them take Cocina. She didn't fight the system for her daughter. She didn't cry and argue and scream like most parents would if someone was taking their child away. Phoenix simply moved out of their way. With a stern face, she reminded herself she was making the right decision. Elise had never given Phoenix away. She kept her locked up for thirteen years. She believed Cocina deserved a better Mom than her. *Cocina would thank me one day,* Phoenix told herself. So, she let them take Cocina and didn't fight to get her back.

Phoenix peeked at Cocina. Her daughter, her youngest child. Whom she failed to protect. Failed to show love. Cocina was a walking billboard for everything she had done wrong.

A roaring sound erupted from Phoenix's body, and she began wailing. One by one, Cocina, Blair, Khalil, Raven, Phoenix, and Carter broke down. The family sobbed as Phoenix put the puzzle together and realized that she was the missing piece.

"I didn't realize how things affected you guys and how it affected Carter. Even Ray. . ." Phoenix said with sad eyes. "I tried to bury those years. Forget them, really. I didn't realize I left you behind in the process. I always thought, '*At least I'll be a good Nana.*' I'm so sorry, so deeply sorry."

"There's still time to be a good mom and a good Nana," Carter whispered. Everyone looked at him, surprised.

"My babies," Nana whimpered, facing Cocina and Khalil. "If you'll let me. If we can try, I'd like to try and be a good mom. Again."

Cocina and Phoenix were already embracing when Phoenix whimpered to her children. The trio stood and held each other. Raven noted this was the first time she ever saw her dad and

Nana embrace. Mom, son, and daughter stood there, together, seeing each other clearly for the first time. Emotions were high in the room as love won above all. It made Raven's heart smile.

"Excellent work Ms. Phoenix." Ms. Margaret clapped. "Thank you for being present and not shutting down. We all want to work together to preserve this family. Khalil, forgive yourself for not knowing better at the time. Forgive your mother and father for not knowing better at the time. Phoenix, forgive yourself for not knowing better at the time. Forgive yourself for survival skills that you picked up along the way to help you endure trauma. Forgive yourself for being who you needed to be to survive. That person is healing now. That person is smarter, wiser, and healthier. You can let that person grow and then let that person go. Let the younger generation decide who they want to become. Let's break those patterns and cycles that we've held on to for so long. We're holding on while our hands are bleeding; it's so much easier to let go. Our own healing is sometimes the most powerful legacy we can gift to our children. Let's recreate your family story. We didn't come from broken families; we came from traumatized families. But now we know better, and we are forging a fresh path. You heal, you grow. You keep healing and growing. People think once you do the work, it's like an arrow, and you shoot straight to the top. Healing is not linear, there are lines all over the place. The commitment to it is what counts. What is it you want for your family? If that's a relationship you care about — you talk to them people with some love in your words and your heart at all times. Hear them out and be gentle with them as they rediscover parts of themselves. We heal us right here. By doing the work and committing to making each other better. Holding each other accountable."

The Jamison's hung onto her every word.

"All right, family, we have one more." Ms. Margaret turned her head. "Carter?"

The family turned to Carter nervously.

"Ray . . . At first, I didn't think she liked me when I got here. But then I thought, '*I did just show up on her doorstep.*'" The family laughed, their eyes glistening. "But she's cool. She's funny and smart. I don't know. When she's around, I feel like things will just be ok," he replied.

Raven's eyes misted. Carter leaned towards her. "I swear I won't come into the bathroom while you're in there ever again. That was not for me to see," he smirked.

Raven's wet eyes widened, and Khalil wrinkled his nose. Phoenix also looked confused.

"What's this about?" Khalil quizzed with wide eyes, "What did you see?" Raven grabbed a pillow and whacked Carter with it as he ducked underneath her swings. He giggled.

"Nothing, Dad — nothing!" Raven talked fast, eyeing Ms. Margaret to continue.

"You did an outstanding job, family, give it up for yourselves. We break generational curses right now. We communicate. We have tough conversations. We make us better by building each other up. This is your tribe." Ms. Margaret looked at each of us. "No one gets left behind. You hear me? No one."

Raven looked around the room at everyone now running through a range of emotions. Some joking, some still crying. Everyone looked a little bit lighter. Raven thought about Amir's family and the pride in his face when he spoke of them. She hoped maybe she could experience that someday soon.

CHAPTER 31

Nia and Raven got on the bus that afternoon, expecting to see Ms. Twizz, but she wasn't there. Someone new was in her place picking them up. Ms. Twizz usually mentioned when she would be absent. The girls shared a glance, confused. It was cold that December and Raven saw Mr. Gerald outside hanging Christmas decorations. She waved to him as she and Nia walked. When they made it over The Hill, Ms. Tina's car was parked in front of Raven's house. That was strange too, as it was only three o'clock. Raven thought about Carter and hoped nothing was wrong. She hurried her pace and tried not to overreact. She quickly opened the front door with her key, and soon she heard laughter with glasses clinking.

"Finally, our girls are home!" Blair exclaimed.

"Is everything okay?"

"Everything is great," Ms. Tina beamed. "We just got word that the State of Louisiana Appeals Court has agreed to hear Ms. Twizz's son's case again. It looks like we really might have a chance to get him out this time."

The girls squealed, and tears pooled in Raven's eyes once again. She just couldn't stop the waterworks these days. She thought about Ms. Twizz and her determination to fight for her family. She never gave up, and for that reason, her son really had another chance at life. Raven's heart burst with happiness for Ms. Twizz. Nia and Raven grinned while Ms. Tina and Blair danced in place and sipped wine.

Raven remembered that night at Nia's house with Ms. Twizz. The girls had discussed the conversation later, and sure enough, Ms. Twizz's words had affected Nia too; she had touched them both. She was getting exactly what she wanted; a second chance. Ms. Twizz had lit a fire under Raven by telling her story. Life seemed so much different after Raven processed her words. *Be better, fight for your family,* Ms. Twizz had said. Raven had work to do, and she planned to do it. She was thrilled for Ms. Twizz.

"I guess that's why she wasn't on the bus this afternoon," Raven recalled.

"She's probably down at the station filling out some paperwork. I'm just so happy, I can't believe we really got this done." Ms. Tina was in happy shock.

"You did this girl, you did this!" Blair danced in front of Ms. Tina. They hugged and poured more wine.

"Can we have some?" Nia eyeballed the wine glass — trying her luck. "Girl — get out my face." Ms. Tina shooed Nia away.

They giggled.

Raven looked at them — Blair and Ms. Tina. Even Ms. Twizz was in her thoughts. Three brown moms. Three brown girls. They helped each other; they stood by each other. They were women who never gave up and who never backed down. They just keep on keeping on.

Raven wondered if she and Nia would be the same way when they were their ages. They had to be, they had too many great examples for it to be any other way.

Later that night, after Nia went home, Raven started her homework. She had been putting it off for a while, and even though she had a pleasant afternoon, it was still in the back of her mind.

Her *Who I Am?* project was due in a few days. Ms. Whitaker and Raven hadn't even started piecing it together. She collected trinkets, magazines, different clippings, and articles for the past few weeks. She sat on her bedroom floor with her items strewn about and got started. She cut out a bunch of pictures she thought represented her the most. Sunflowers, music symbols, dancers. There was even a picture of Misty Copeland that she had to have. There was a picture of sorority sisters all dressed up in their matching jackets. It made Raven think of her Brown Girls Club jackets she and her friends wore. She smiled, looking at it, and placed it on her poster board. She saw a picture of Jackson State University and paused. She thought about college and if that was something she still wanted to do. She wasn't so sure anymore. Raven had encouraged Amir to follow his dreams beyond basketball, and maybe Raven needed to take her own advice.

She had her *'thing'* all along.

Everyone else saw it when she danced. Maybe it was time Raven took herself seriously. She took out her phone and googled the Alvin Ailey Dance Academy. Raven printed out a picture and placed it on her board next to her picture of Jackson State. They still had a bomb dance team, and she couldn't rule them out either.

Just maybe.

Raven found hearts and different things relating to love. This was her second time doing this project, and she thought back to the first one. She put nothing about love on that one. It wasn't something that she had even thought about. This time Raven thought about Amir and their friendship. She glued a heart down onto the poster board. She found different pictures of families, some with same-sex parents, some with pets, some White, some Black. She cut out a few pictures of Black families and pasted them on her poster board in the center.The center of her world was currently her family. She scrolled through her phone, looking for a picture of her poster board from last year. She stopped scrolling when she found it. She enlarged it and zoomed in to get a better look. Raven had a picture of her family on the old poster, but it wasn't in the center, and it wasn't displayed like it should have been. She knew better this time.

Next, she glued the picture right in the center where it belonged. She arranged everything else in various shapes and poses around that one picture. Raven filled up the board with more and more articles, poems, pictures, and she even drew a couple herself with some markers. She did everything she could to fill it up and made some pictures overlap others. But that's how Raven saw her life these days anyway; everything bled together, and nothing was in its own box or in its own place. Everything overlapped and touched. Just like in real life. And she was managing it all and not doing half bad — if she said so herself.

Finally, the board was complete. It felt like Raven, it looked like Raven. She grinned at it.

Raven again compared it to her poster from last year. These posters were almost exactly one year apart, and yet they described two different people. Raven couldn't wait to show Ms. Whitaker.

CHAPTER 32

When the last bell rang, Raven stopped in to see Ms. Whitaker before she met Amir to set up for their project. She wanted to show Ms. Whitaker her *Who I Am?* board. Raven and Ms. Whitaker almost ran smack into each other in her office doorway; She walked in, and Ms. Whitaker's head was down as she walked out. They almost crashed into each other.

"Raven! I'm so sorry, are you okay?" Ms. Whitaker held Raven's shoulders as they bumped. Raven bounced back into the wall.

"I'm okay, it's okay."

Ms. Whitaker pulled Raven from the wall and ushered her into her office. She sat down in front of Ms. Whitaker's desk as she handed her a bottle of water. She cracked it open as Ms. Whitaker sat down.

"So, what's up, Ms. Raven? You came all this way to see your favorite school counselor?" she said with a half smirk. Raven whipped out her poster board and showed it to Ms. Whitaker. Taking it in her hands, Ms. Whitaker studied it. She looked at each picture carefully, her eyes roamed around the board. Raven used each item to piece together a story. The story of Raven Jamison and all the things that made Raven-Raven. Ms. Whitaker sat the board down and looked at her for a while. She smiled. Raven beamed back. They grinned at each other, each of them understanding what that moment meant. Ms. Whitaker spoke first.

“Raven, how far we’ve come.”

“I know, what a mess,” Raven quipped. She threw her head back and touched her forehead in dramatic fashion. She was her father’s child.

Ms. Whitaker laughed.

Raven felt the word vomit rise in her. She was getting more used to it these days, and sometimes she surprised herself with what came out of her mouth. She recognized the feeling these days. It seemed like it happened so much more. She was getting less anxious about expressing herself and speaking up on things that bothered her. It was an uncomfortable feeling, but one that she was not shying away from any longer.

“Ms. Whitaker,” Raven started. “I wanted to show you my poster, but I also wanted to talk to you about what I said in our last session. About me reading what you wrote on your notepad.”

Ms. Whitaker sat back in her seat. Her eyes softened.

Raven continued.

“It bothered me, and I didn’t want to come back to therapy. I thought about telling my mom to sign me out of the group. But this year, I felt alone on an island. Or even sometimes that I was in a room full of people, but no one heard me or saw me. I even preferred it that way. To not be seen. I just want you to know. . . I'm sorry for bringing it up the way I did. That wasn't fair. You weren't right about your assessment, but you weren't wrong either. I could see why you came to that assumption."

Ms. Whitaker's eyes watered. Raven handed her a tissue from her own desk. She didn't let a tear drop.

"I'm sorry you saw that Ms. Raven," she said, and then went on to explain. "I'm really sorry. I've thought about this since you mentioned it. As a counselor, it's never my intention for you to see session notes written on my desk. I'm glad you told me. It's made me more diligent about keeping my areas clean. Thank you for being honest with me. I have to make clinical assessments, and sometimes it doesn't capture who someone really is."

Raven didn't want her to feel bad. She just wanted Ms. Whitaker to know she was more than what she or anyone said she was. But she was still thankful for Ms. Whitaker. She didn't give up on Raven, and she showed her all those Black faces on her office walls. Raven looked over Ms. Whitaker's shoulders to her wall of pictures and noticed a picture of Ms. Whitaker and her boyfriend. They were smiling together, cheek to cheek. Raven observed Ms. Whitaker's wall many times and never saw that picture.

Raven thought of Amir. Funny how you didn't see love until it saw you.

The after-school bell rang, and Raven rushed from Ms. Whitaker's office and met Amir at the chemistry lab early to set up for their project. She set up all the materials, including the cups, sugar, and salt. Amir began writing in their team notebook so they could record all details. She looked around the room, sizing up the competition.

The first team was Brianna and Randy, and they wore matching t-shirts. Brian wore an 'O', and Randy wore an 'MG,' but as symbols from the periodic table. When they stood together, they spelled, "OMG." *Damn,* Raven thought. She and Amir could have thought of that. She tried to focus on their project and not their shirts; they built a robot and used coding to make it fly a drone around the chemistry lab. It was very entertaining, and the room seemed fascinated by it as the drone whizzed by their heads. It dipped lower and higher; every time it moved and flew. Mr. Fritzel seemed to jump in place, and he was clearly amused — Raven watched him intently. She wasn't feeling too confident with their water and sugar trick.

Racquel and her partner, John, were up next. They built a lawnmower from scrap parts. Amir and Raven watched Racquel and John break the entire piece down and show them item by item how they could rebuild it. Although it was not as powerful as a regular lawnmower, it still worked. They dazzled Raven herself.

"Very nice work, Ms. Jones and Mr. Richter." Mr. Fritzel wrote something down and peered up from his glasses.

They did not come to play today.

Amir must have been thinking the same thing because he looked at her with a strange face. A face that said, *'We're going up against drones and lawnmowers with water and ice.'*

They said nothing, but they shared a laugh at the irony. Raven tried to calm her nerves and prepare for the massacre about to happen. She scanned the room, searching for five things. Raven took one last deep breath before Amir said,

"You ready for this?"

Normally she would have found some way to back out of it. Feign sick. Bad nerves. But today, she already accepted that they had lost the competition before it even started. She and Amir had the worst project up there. It wasn't bad, but up against the other two options — they already knew what was about to happen.

And the thing is ...

She was okay with it. Looking at Amir and being there with him felt like she had already won. She knew that they would be okay.

"Ms. Jamison and Mr. Ferguson — go."

"Go," Mr. Fritzel had said. He was still throwing them a little shade for having their water fight a couple weeks ago. Although he didn't report it to administration, he could have. Raven was thankful he didn't, so she accepted his attitude. Raven and Amir poured water over seven different ice baths in Styrofoam cups. Amir walked back and forth, studying each cup for imperfections. Raven replenished the water in each as needed and held the stopwatch. As soon as the ice bath dropped to −10°C, Raven added more ice water like they practiced. She walked around and labeled each of the Styrofoam cups, so they knew which beaker held which solution. She poured water into the beaker with the salt. She stirred it with a rod until all the ice crystals dissolved. Raven checked the temperature of each beaker, and Amir scribbled down the cup numbers. They checked and rechecked the tubes. They hadn't thought this thing through.

The first two practice runs only took about twenty minutes when they practiced it. *Or had they?* Raven pondered. She and Amir spent most of their chemistry lab time talking and joking around. Maybe it took longer, and they hadn't noticed. She wasn't sure. The other groups did all their work on the front end. Raven and Amir's ice project took upwards of an hour. She looked at the stopwatch again; it would be a slow experiment, and she hoped Mr. Fritzel would be okay with it.

He seemed to be most excited by the quick 'crack crack boom' experiments. Raven thought about his squeal when Racquel's lawnmower roared to life. After about fifteen minutes, they saw crystals form on their tests.

Thank God.

Amir and Raven walked around each of the beakers, studying them. Sure enough, after some time, the crystals had frozen, just like they did for Raven and Amir the first time. People were halfway falling asleep by the time it finished. Mr. Fritzel glanced at his watch a few times and sighed every five minutes. Around the ten-minute mark, he took out a pen and word puzzle.

Amir cleared his throat. "As you can see, using minimal materials, you can successfully lower the temperature of water and create ice. This can be used when camping or in situations when you don't have many items. Thank you." He finished by taking a bow before anyone even clapped.

Raven also took a bow with him.

They stood side by side; his hand touched hers again. They were both trying not to laugh. She knew they would pass the class, but they had bombed the project. Amir seemed to be okay with it too, holding back a snort.

"Is that it?" Mr. Fritzel put away his word puzzle.

"Umm, yes. Yes, it is" Raven cleared her throat.

"Thank you for that, ugh. . . engaging display of water, Ms. Jamison." Amir's snort had escaped him, and he giggled. She held back her own laughter and prayed that Mr. Fritzel didn't notice.

"Okay, team, let's cast our votes."

The room went around and voted on their favorite project. Mr. Fritzel gathered the votes, and he divided them up and counted. He turned around as anxious eyes watched on. "First place, Brianna and Randy." Brianna and Randy cheered as they accepted their certificate. "Second place is John and Racquel." John and Racquel accepted their certificate, but by this time, Amir and Raven clearly knew they were in third place. They fell into a fit of giggles. "Anddd to the surprise of no one, Raven and Amir took third place for their ice trick." Raven went up and accepted their certificate.

"Thank you, Mr. Fritzel," Raven said sweetly. She turned around and crossed her eyes at Amir. He couldn't hold it and cackled. They had lost the chemistry battle, but there was an ever-growing chemistry between the two of them.

CHAPTER 33

The Brown Girls Club sat in the bleachers Friday night at Lake Lacroix High School to watch Amir on the floor getting blown out. He was doing his best to carry the team, but nothing appeared to be helping. Raven peered out the windows during the game. She was thrilled the weather had warmed again to the sixties — a normal Louisiana December heading into the holidays.

Raven sat at the top of the bleachers cackling with her girls. Although she watched the game, she really just watched Amir. The rest of the assault was painful to watch, but you just couldn't look away. The team was just awful, there was no way around it. She could see Amir's frustration building from the stands, and whenever the opposing team made a basket, she winced for him. Amir's team missed free throws and layups. When the other team made baskets and ran back down to the other end of the court, Amir's team walked back. He spotted her in the crowd and waved. She waved back. Taylor looked over and scowled. Raven looked around for Justin and soon spotted

him in the crowd a few feet from Taylor. He limped and wore a boot on his foot. Justin walked towards Taylor and placed his arm around her shoulder; she slipped out of his embrace.

Raven turned her attention back to the game. That wasn't her business.

"Do you guys want to go grab pizza after the game?" Trinity asked. "I'm out, I got to do something with my mom," Nia said.

"I'm out too," Jasmine mumbled. "I don't have a ride home, and my dad isn't letting me borrow the car anymore." Their eyes got big as they looked away, recalling their fateful driving adventure.

"I'm down," Raven answered. Everyone turned and looked at her. "You want to go?" Jasmine sat wide eyed.

"Yeah, I can go," Raven repeated.

The final buzzer rang, and the game was over. Amir's team was beat by double digits. The other team clapped and cheered for one another while Amir's team sullenly walked back to the locker room.

"Hey, Amir!" Raven ran down the bleachers. "You want to grab some pizza after this?"

"Sure." He wiped sweat from his forehead with a towel. "You going to Lake Lacroix Pizza?"

"Yeah. I'll meet you there in about an hour."

Amir shook his head and walked into the locker room.

Raven ran back up to the girls, "Amir is coming too."

Trinity peeked at her incredulously. "Who is this woman? This isn't Raven." Trinity glanced towards the sky as if she was seeking answers.

Raven giggled to herself and said nothing. Trinity and Raven waited for Nia and Jasmine to leave before they walked the short distance to the pizza shop. It wasn't far from school, and they often strolled there during lunch breaks. Raven's phone buzzed, and she swiped up to see who it was.

Amir: *I'm here*

Raven picked up her pace, wondering how he beat her there. She didn't see him come out of the locker room with the rest of the team. Trinity took a phone call as they trekked, and she got louder and louder on the phone. She hung up. "Ray, you're going to kill me, I have to go home. My dad needs me to stay at the house until the contractor's leave."

"We have to tell Amir we're not coming." Raven stopped walking.

"Not we — me. I'm not coming." Trinity corrected. "You still go."

Raven was thoughtful. She hadn't factored her and Amir alone in a pizza shop, just the two of them. Sure, he came to her house a few times, but that was to study. There would be no studying tonight. Raven wondered if she should cancel.

Trinity said in a low voice, "Ray, just go. It's just pizza. You'll be fine."

Raven glanced at Trinity. She was the shortest of the girls standing at five-foot-even, and she was always so calm. She admired that about Trinity. She was right; it would be okay. Raven started moving again in the direction of the pizza shop.

"I'll catch up with you later," she said, turning in the opposite direction of Trinity.

Trinity jumped in place. "You got this Ray, text if you need me." She squealed.

Raven took a deep breath and pressed forward.

Amir was already waiting inside for Raven when she arrived. "I hear it's just me and you today," he said with a smile. Trinity must have texted him and told him she couldn't stay.

And he still came, Raven inferred.

"Can we get a table for two?" Amir leaned over the counter, motioning to the server. They escorted Amir and Raven to their table, and they sat quietly, staring at their menus. Her hands were sweaty.

"I'm sorry about the game," she said, looking up from her menu. She wasn't sure why she was studying the menu. They were in a pizza shop, and she was getting pizza. She put the menu down and played with her straw.

"I'm not worried about that, it'll come together in time."

"You're so calm about it. If I got beat by twenty plus points, I'd at least have an attitude."

"Oh, you got jokes" he shot a paper straw at Raven. They laughed. "How is your dad?" Amir asked.

Khalil came to the school the week before and did his yearly 'don't do drugs and use condoms' speech. Amir and Khalil struck up a conversation. Amir came to the house a few times before, and he and Khalil didn't speak much. Now they thought they were friends. Raven couldn't explain it.

"He's okay," Raven told him about the latest with Carter.

"You're always in my business, what's going on with you? She quizzed. Amir sat back in the booth. "I'm making it."

"What's that mean?"

He shrugged his shoulders

"Talk to me. I'm ready for you to lie on my couch and tell me all your secrets," she joked.

He smiled.

"I've just been thinking about the school. We moved here to help my chances of getting a basketball scholarship. The way these games have been looking, I don't know if that will even happen." His eyes were lost. He scanned the restaurant and landed on everything but her.

Blair always says when a Black man shares his innermost thoughts with you, you listen.

Raven listened.

"My entire future depends on me getting a scholarship. I don't like that. I think I'm pretty good at other things too. But everyone wants me to shut up and dribble. What if I don't want to dribble? What if I want to own the team or manage behind the scenes?"

"Those are all great options, Amir. What stops you?"

"Me. I guess me."

"Then stop your shit. You can do all of those things. You can play basketball, own the team, and you do whatever you want to do. You don't have to be what everyone else wants you to be." The words flowed out of Raven with no effort. It was so easy to see someone else's problems clearly, yet she struggled to apply them to her own life. "You just have to do it. Once you make a choice, the people around you will support you and fall in line. You don't have to be there to support and hold them up all the time. You can just be what you're ready to be — when you're ready to be it." Raven tried to comfort him as best as she could and as he had done for her. She lowered her voice like she saw her mom do with her dad. Raven looked at Amir square in the eyes. She let him talk and lay down whatever was on his mind. It felt good to be there for him the way he had been for her the past few months.

"Dr. Ray," Amir bantered. "Is everything okay with you and Taylor?" Raven stopped laughing. "Yea, I think so. Why?"

"No reason, I saw her looking at you at the game tonight."

"I think she saw me looking at you."

"Why were you looking at me?"

Raven's face felt flush. "Because. . . you were getting beat so bad tonight I had to make sure you were okay."

Amir spit out some of his soda he was sipping and laughed. He shot another paper straw in her direction.

"But seriously, you good?"

Raven quieted, and a flurry of thoughts ran through her mind. *Was I good?* She wasn't sure. She probed her feelings, and before she knew it, the word vomit came back. She told Amir everything. Raven detailed her time with Taylor and Ms. Whitaker, her family's session together, getting her nails done by Aunt Cocina. She even told him she requested an information packet from the Alvin Ailey Dance Academy in New York. Raven didn't tell anyone that yet.

And Amir. Amir told Raven about his mom and being there for his younger sister. Amir watched a few documentaries about sports agents, and he admitted he was interested in learning more about it. But everyone saw a tall, young Black man, and they told him what he was supposed to be. He was unsure how to show others anyone else.

Raven and Amir shared pizza, time, and understanding. One by one, the lights in the pizza shop shut off — and the server returned to their table. "Hey guys, we're closing in thirty minutes. Just a heads up," she said, clearly annoyed. She walked away in a huff.

Raven looked around. They were the only ones left and had stayed until closing. Raven looked at her phone and had three missed calls. One from Trinity and two from Blair. She had only one text message from Blair.

Blair: *I know how to track your phone now, girl. You make me come down to that pizza shop in my slippers, and that's your ass.*

"Oh, crap, it's getting late. My mom is looking for me," Raven grabbed a to-go box. They went through two pizzas while sitting there talking.

"How are you getting home?" he asked.

"I was going to take an Uber."

"I'll share one with you." Amir got up and paid the bill at the register. While he paid, Raven ordered a ride through her Uber app. They headed outside to wait for their car to arrive. It was a warmer night, and Raven wore a light windbreaker and Amir, a basketball hoodie.

Once their car arrived, they piled into the back seat and sat next to each other. Their driver hit a bump in the road, and Raven's arm bumped Amir's. Her left hand was down on the seat. He moved his hand closer to hers. They touched.

Amir gazed at Raven.

She gazed at him.

He opened his mouth to say something but stopped. No words came out.

His head moved closer to Raven's, and her heart began beating.

She moved her head away and inched back. Amir retreated and gave Raven space — letting her choose. She moved closer to Amir and placed her hand over top of his. Amir leaned forward and touched the side of her cheek, and kissed her softly on the lips.

He pulled back, his eyes searched Raven's. Raven wasn't sure how long they sat there kissing. Their Uber driver cleared his throat and eyed them from the rearview mirror. "We're at the first destination," he reported. Raven opened her eyes and untangled herself from Amir.

Physically and emotionally.

Raven saw Blair standing in the front doorway of their house. The porch light was on, and she was in her house robe with curlers in her hair, tapping her foot and looking at her watch. It was 11:11 p.m. *Gofigure,* Raven mused. Raven could see Blair's ratty old nightgown from the car.

Amir spotted her and smirked.

"See you tomorrow?" He asked.

“Tomorrow,” Raven said slowly and closed the door.

CHAPTER 34

Blair and Khalil sat up front. Cocina and Phoenix in the back, Raven, moderating between them. D'Angelo crooned on the radio about brown sugar. There was a light chill clinging to the windows. Khalil fumbled with the controls, trying to keep the windows defrosted. Phoenix nodded her head and sang along to the music. Cocina sat on the other side, biting her nails in the back.

It was officially Christmas time. That meant a host of eggnog, ham, turkey, cookies, pies, macaroni and cheese, sauerkraut, crawfish, collard greens, beans, rice, jambalaya, and Po-Boys. Along with the food came the family events.

This was their first problem, Raven mused. They didn't have to worry about Thanksgiving. Carter went with his mom, Phoenix was with Johnny Gil, and the Jamison family had a small — impromptu dinner. Christmas was a big one, and Raven wondered what it would look like this year.

The family was on their way to Carter's school, and he was performing in his Christmas concert. Blair dropped him off earlier in the day with the rest of the students to practice before the big show.

Raven wasn't sure when it had happened. . . she couldn't remember one specific date or time it occurred. She just knew that

Carter was different. His shift made the rest of the house shift. As the days and weeks went on, he became. . . tolerable. She noticed little things at first. He wasn't hoarding food in his room anymore. Then he began taking part in family discussions.

One night for Huddle, his high and low was the same.

That he lived with us.

The calls from school became less frequent. He had improved, his school agreed. Conversations about school expulsion ceased. He came back from his sessions with Ms. Margaret upbeat, sometimes even laughing.

It was a sight to see.

Raven pondered the change. Everyone was running on all cylinders these days. Blair went back to the gallery to work a couple days per week. She was animated when she returned home for the day with reports of news from Lake Lacroix. Khalil was there too — cracking his jokes through it all. He started picking up Carter every day from school; he said they talked a lot on their rides home. Khalil was taking him fishing this weekend.

Raven looked around at her family in the car. Everyone was so wrapped in their own thoughts. They looked nervous, but everyone expressed it differently. These people had never, not one time, been in the car together like this. Carter had also brought 'em out. Raven continued running numbers and assessing what could go wrong in her head.

Blair squealed from the front seat, "Yes, this is my jam!" she turned up the music. Mary J. Blige bellowed from the radio. Phoenix joined in, nodding her head, and before long, Aunt Cocina's voice was heard from the back. Her rich tone was heavy; she sang from her soul. Raven stopped singing to listen to her.

"You are the one for me," Aunt Cocina sang. Raven watched her mom, Aunt Cocina, and grandmother croon together, and soon they heard a deep, baritone voice which belonged to Khalil, chime in.

He turned to Blair as he drove, and he sang to her. The car shrieked in laughter, pulling up to the school. Khalil screeched to a halt, and they spilled out of the car — hootin' and hollerin'.

"What?" Khalil eyed a few people they passed walking into the building. There had been lots of stares as they walked in, shoulder to shoulder. Khalil led from the left, Blair to his right, Phoenix to her right, Cocina was next, and Raven closed the Jamison line. Khalil felt powerful with the ladies by his side. He looked at them as allies, fighting together in their generational trauma war. Blair wore a 'Protect Black Women' sweater to the concert.

He intended to do just that.

Khalil grabbed his wife's hand and tucked his fingers between hers. He greeted a coworker standing off to the side with his own family. Khalil introduced everyone for the first time.

Khalil proudly said, “This is my mom,” and Nana blinked back tears.

“I'll be right back,” Cocina headed to the bathroom.

“Hold on, I'm coming too.” Raven walked beside Cocina.

“Let me see them nails, girl.” Cocina huffed. She examined Raven's nails and flung them back, looking at her through the bathroom mirror. “I told you to stop messing with them gels and get you some dip powder!” she declared.

Cocina was the nail guru.

“Well, how about you hook me up, Aunt CoCo?”

“I don't do nothin' for free. Black women should never do nothin' for free. But I'll give you the family discount,” she winked.

Khalil was tapping his foot and chewing the inside of his mouth as he held two seats for Cocina and Raven. He exhaled when he spotted them walking towards him, giggling to themselves. It made his heart smile to see them sharing a laugh.

“Over here!” He waved his hand.

“Excuse me, excuse me,” Raven and Cocina scooted in front of others in their row to get to their seats. “Finally! Y'all made it, I was getting worried ya'll were getting jumped in the bathroom or something," Khalil chuckled. Blair swatted his leg with the program. Cocina laughed.

Raven looked around the room and spotted Ms. Twizz and her grandson, RJ. "He should be getting out real soon," Ms. Twizz told her a few weeks ago. "It would be the best Christmas gift. There's a good chance this time." Nia's mom said it was 'prosecutorial misconduct' after they were permitted to reintroduce evidence. They were expecting a full release.

Raven waved to her. She hoped she'd get her Christmas gift this year. Raven was surrounded by so many competent and strong Black women she didn't have any other option but to soar herself like her name implied.

The lights dimmed, and everyone took their seats. The room hushed, and music played from the brightly lit stage. The first class came out and sang 'Jingle Bell Rock.' It was cute. Raven guessed Ms. Twizz's other grandson was in that class because she was snapping all kinds of pictures and went live on Facebook. Raven giggled to herself as she watched Ms. Twizz navigate Facebook. She pressed a bunch of buttons on her phone and bit her lip. The font on her phone was super big, and Raven could see all the icons from their row.

Carter's class was up next. He walked onto the stage, following in a single line behind other students. He was small for his age. Raven saw Cocina's knuckles latch onto the seat as she sat up in her chair to get a better look. He was wearing grey Vans and blue jeans. Raven couldn't make out his sweater from here as she squinted her eyes.

Swiss Miss.

A mug.

Cocoa.

He was wearing a cup of cocoa as his sweater. Cocoa for his CoCo. Cocina bit her lip and peered down the aisle to Blair. She blinked back tears and looked between her sister-in-law and the stage. They stared at each other. Four eyes connected between them. Blair would always have her back too.

The class sang 'Frosty the Snowman,' and they struggled to warm up. Everyone, including Carter, mumbled the words.

"You got this Car!" Cocina screamed out. He beamed with pride and sang louder, which made the other students sing louder too. As Carter led the pack in singing, his teacher turned the mic towards him. He half sang, half-rapped 'Frosty the Snowman.' Students behind Carter nodded their heads and snapped their fingers in approval. As the song ended and a new one started up, and he led his troops in a rendition of 'I Saw Mommy Kissing Santa Claus.' Cocina leaned past Raven in the aisle and said to her family, "He probably did!" She slapped her knee and laughed while Khalil roared with amusement from his seat. For the second time that night,

Carter saw his family laugh from the audience. He sang even louder. While the others continued to joke, Cocina looked at her son. Her only child. He stood on the stage and danced in a way she had never seen before. He smiled, wriggled his nose when he was supposed to, and made silly faces with others.

He looked like a child.

Cocina noted all the times he didn't look like a child to her. All the times, he had to be a grown-up for her. Cocina only remembered harder faces. Eyebrows furrowed; head dropped. She hadn't seen these laughs and giggles since Carter was a baby.

Cocina felt like a truck had hit her. She looked over at Blair and Khalil, who both watched and cheered on Carter from their seats. They brought out this side of him. He was up there smiling for them. Cocina grabbed her jacket from behind the auditorium chair and thought about running. Carter didn't need her, she processed. Cocina didn't notice Phoenix watching her from the corner of her eyes. She saw Cocina grab her jacket, and before Cocina could turn to run, she grabbed her hand. They locked eyes amidst the sights and sounds that swirled around them. They saw each other, mother, and daughter. Phoenix's eyes pleaded with Cocina's not to leave. Cocina's stomach churned, and she felt light-headed.

But he doesn't need me, she reflected — pulling her hand away from Phoenix's. Phoenix held Cocina's hand harder. *But he does*, her eyes said. *But he does.* Cocina looked back up at her son. They moved the mic even closer to him, and you could hear more of his singing voice over his classmates. His eyes sparkled with wonder and joy. Cocina looked at him a long time and back at her mom. She released her grip on her jacket and laid it back down. Cocina would be here for every event and every-everything. All ways and always. Phoenix's eyes softened as Cocina waved the white flag and placed her jacket back over the chair. With no words spoken between them, they had an entire conversation. Cocina glanced over at the rest of the family and chuckled. Blair, Khalil, and Raven cheered for Carter from their seats. They didn't even notice Cocina and Phoenix. The song ended, and the kids took a bow. The room erupted with applause. The children on stage congratulated each other. Carter smiled and pointed to Cocina. She beamed and pointed back. She would have been crazy to miss this. Carter ran down from the stage and sprinted to his mother. He embraced her, his small arms not fitting around her waist. Cocina clung to her son and kissed his forehead. The Jamison family exited the school — together.

A ride that began earlier in the day with five nervous family members quietly driving to school concluded with six family members who hugged and joked on their way home together.

They look like a family.

Blair cooked dinner before they left, and once they arrived home, she began dishing out plates of food. Carter set the table, Phoenix and Cocina made plates, and everyone talked and joked.

"Alexa, play Slide by H.E.R," Blair called out.

Music filled the dining room, and Cocina danced with Carter and Raven.

"Let me see what you got girl, I heard you got my moves," Cocina teased.

"It's actually my moves!" Khalil huffed.

Raven stood next to her aunt, and they both began to dance. Carter joined in the center and began shaking his legs and arms until they all burst out laughing.

There was a soft knock on the door, and Raven heard Nia before she saw her. She crooned to the song shimmying into the room. Not far behind her was Ms. Tina and Bryce. Blair must have invited them, Raven thought, as Nia brushed past her with a wink.

"Hey, Bryce!" Carter said. They went to school together, and Carter said he was cool — so he was cool.

"I brought wine," Ms. Tina handed a bottle to Blair. They helped Carter finish setting the table, and when finished, he sat down next to his mom and scooted his chair closer to her. She leaned into him, and they began whispering.

"All right, all right, enough of that," Khalil carried a large pot into the dining room. Blair followed with more pots and Ms. Tina with the wine. The family sat around the table, steam from the hot pots rose, and fresh aromas from the food wafted through the air. Plates were swapped, glasses clinked, and food was everywhere. Rice, gumbo, bread, salad, crawfish, vegetables, corn, potatoes. Raven wondered when her mom had the time to do all of this as she looked around the table. Blair popped the wine bottle open and began pouring. She passed the bottle to Cocina. Cocina declined.

"Lagniappe," Khalil said, shoveling food into his mouth.

"Your NOLA twang is still there, Lil," Phoenix was amused. She hadn't heard him say that word in a while. He used to always say it as a child when he ate something superb.

"Pinch the tail, suck the head, Lil! I know you can do better than that!" Cocina said to Khalil as crawfish juice dribbled down his mouth.

"Mind your business!" He retorted.

"Anyone up for Huddle?" Blair looked around.

"What's that?" Ms. Tina asked.

"They go around the table and talk about their positives and negatives from the day," Nia explained.

"I'll go first, I'll go it first," Blair said. "My high was Carter. I loved seeing you up there singing and dancing. I don't have any lows today. Not a single one."

"Okay, let me go." Phoenix sat up straight. "My high was also getting to see my grandson happy. My low. . . I'm not sure, I don't think I have one either," she nodded at Blair.

Ms. Tina cleared her throat.

"I have news. Miss Simone-"

"No, Mom, it's Ms. Twizz!" Nia corrected.

"I'm sorry, girl, Ms. Twizz! Anyway — they held a hearing today, and they're going to move forward with a conditional release for her son. I just got the call and figured I would come over with wine! So, no lows for me either!"

The table roared with happiness.

"I'll drink to that!" Phoenix smiled.

"Now that's a high," Blair and Ms. Tina clinked glasses.

"Me next." Raven offered. "My high is also Carter today. But my high lately has been Carter," she glanced at him as she spoke.

"Any lows?" Nana asked.

"Nope, not one for me."

Nia and Bryce took turns. Nia was excited that she had defended her co-captain spot on the dance team. They had challenged her for her position too. There had been a lot of challenges for them all lately, in more ways than one. Bryce was excited that he and Carter had gym class together. Both had no lows. Cocina shifted in her seat.

"My turn. . . of course it's you, Bug." She turned to Carter as she spoke. "It's always you. And going forward, it will continue to be you. . . when I saw you up there, I was just so proud. And I have another one! I've officially accepted a full-time position at Lake Lacroix Nail Salon. Coco's Cuties coming soon!" She danced in her seat as she shared the last part. "No lows!" Food flew out of her mouth. The family clapped and screamed for her, and she beamed with pride.

"I guess I'm next," Khalil said. "I don't want to be cliché, but my high is the same. Carter. You changed us. You have done this," he looked around the room. "You have all of us now, and we will never let you fall." Everyone at the table nodded in agreement. "And I do have a low I need to discuss. It's pretty serious," he wiped his mouth. "I'd like to apologize for Raven passing gas in the backseat of the car today. I know she smells like zoo dirt."

"Whaaattt!" Raven spit out her juice everywhere. "I did not!" she screamed.

Carter held his side laughing while he tried to wipe away tears from his eyes.

"You go, Carter!" Raven rolled her eyes at her Dad.

Carter spoke. "Well, I think my high is this" he scanned the room. "We never sat down like this. We've never done this. I feel okay." He said it as a matter of fact. Then, as he stole a spoonful of rice said, "I ain't got no low either."

The family eyed Carter. His growth was amazing to witness.

After their intense therapy session, they were different people. Raven looked over at Carter, him and Dad discussing the Saints game. Mom, Nana, and Aunt Coco were trying to learn Tik Tok.

Raven took it all in.

Their family had to be burned down to the ground to be rebuilt. Like a phoenix, they rose. Each of them was a puzzle piece, and in order to see the full picture, those pieces needed to come together. Their glow up had been real, but here they were — doing the work. Raven came from pretty good stock. A line of powerful women who were too legit to ever quit. And they didn't. So, Raven didn't. This season was really personal.

Their family would continue to grow and figure out things together. Cocina stood there clean from drugs. Proud. Ready to face the future. Carter examined his mother, hopeful that this time was different. Somehow, he knew that it would be because this time, he had Uncle Lil on his side. He hadn't had that before.

CHAPTER 35

The family finished dinner and hopped back in the car. They took two vehicles with Nia, Ms. Tina, and Bryce, who followed behind. They rode down Great River Road, and Raven smelled the smoke before she saw it. Her heart skipped a beat. The smoky scent reminded her of when she was a kid, and she used to go see the Christmas bonfires with her parents.

Now they took Carter. He was the first one out of the car and ran up to the structure in amazement. Aunt Cocina was not far behind him and yelled for him to be careful.

There was a cold chill in the air as the families piled out of their cars and exhaled the frigid temperature. Well, the air wasn't really frigid. It was about fifty degrees in Lake Lacroix, but to Lakeans, that was the same as a White Christmas. The Great River Road between New Orleans and Lake Lacroix contained river levees holding back the mighty Mississippi River.

Raven inhaled deeply as soon as she stepped out of the car. Dozens of fifteen-foot-high flaming burning logs stood erected and ablaze. They crafted the mounds into teepee-shapes and shone brightly. Bright orange and red flames danced and crackled around Raven, and she could see the mounds from miles away when they were riding up. Her family usually built their own bonfire, but this year they joined Trinity's family as her brother already built theirs. The families mingled, talked, joked, and laughed. They celebrated the holidays and welcomed Papa Noel as the flames illuminated his trail.

Carter ran around one of the teepees with Bryce. Raven overheard him telling Bryce that his birthday was next month and asked him if he wanted to sleep over. That made Raven smile. Slow and steady it went, slow and steady.

When Blair found out that Carter still believed in Papa Noel and had yet to experience a true Christmas bonfire, she knew they had to take a trip down Great River Road. This was one family tradition Blair remembered fondly with her own parents. Every year they took the ride to see the 'fire tee-pees' as Blair called them as a child. As the story goes that her mom told her: Creole settlers lit bonfires along the Mississippi River days leading up to Christmas to light the way for Papa Noel, the Cajun Santa Claus, along the erected river levees. At dusk, the teepees were doused with lighter fluid and set ablaze, lighting the skies. Families gathered and crowded around the structures. Ant had cooked a ton of food, and he was standing close to the structure and dished out bowls of gumbo to everyone. Raven felt her phone buzz and found a text message from Amir. He was just saying hi. He added heart eyes.

Raven smiled and put her phone back in her pocket. She would text him back later, but first, she enjoyed her family.

She reflected as they continued to talk and eat. She looked around at the women in her family. Each of them so unique and intrinsically tied to each other. This was her bloodline. Her mom was partially right. The family you create is more important than the family you come from. That was a true statement, but she wasn't completely accurate. They had created a new family that now included Cocina and Carter. Healing their family was healing them.

Last week, the entire family came to Nana's last yoga session — Khalil included. Raven felt rested, like she could just *be,* and didn't have to save the world. She would keep her magic tucked away and give herself and her family grace. Grace and space. The grace they needed to feel safe and the space they needed to flourish.

On the other side of the tree stood Phoenix, who watched her family. Their family.

The family that Elise created.

The family that she created.

Phoenix had gotten so much wrong. So many times, she thought she was protecting Khalil and Cocina by staying with their dad. Phoenix saw just how much damage she had done by staying way past the length of the relationship's time. But now, as she observed her family, she was reminded of Cocina's words weeks before when they had their first session with Ms. Margaret. Phoenix could still be a good mom and a good nana. And that was her plan.

For so long, Phoenix viewed her mom as complicit in her trauma. Elise never talked about her thoughts or feelings. She was never a hand holding, coddling type of mother. Phoenix spent her entire life harboring anger towards Elise for things she either didn't know or swept under the rug. Elise did what she had to do at the time for survival, just as Phoenix had done and learned to do.

Well, the rug had been pulled back, and all the family dirt was being cleaned out. Phoenix understood her own mother in a way that she had never before. They were not weak women. They did the best they could with the knowledge and understanding of the world they had at the time. Each woman had sacrificed and given up so much for their family, for future generations, and more to come. They were women who did what they had to do at a time when women had to fight for everything they had.

Even respect from a man.

Phoenix looked around and saw Blair and Khalil looking around, doing the same. They saw it too — no, they felt it. The magic happening between them all. They were the Jamison family.

Future ancestors.

A family rediscovering themselves and each other. Forgiving each other and building bridges. Together.

The end

Thank you for reading "Hey, Brown Girl." I'd love to hear what you think! If you enjoyed this book (or even if you didn't), please visit the site where you purchased it and write a brief review. Your feedback is so important to me and will help other readers decide whether to read the book too.

If you enjoy young adult stories about melanated characters navigating love, friendships, and family, please consider sticking around for my collection of words. Watch me make a SCENE!

PS: Check out the next page for a sneak peek into my next novel, *"Forty-Two Minutes"* coming soon June 2021.

Forty-Two Minutes

"Fuck," I exclaimed out loud, glancing around the room. My breath was ragged and my heartbeat in my ears. *Think, Indigo, think,* I whispered to myself. The incinerator was still running, it's loud hum reminded me of easier times. Easier times like an hour ago. Could that be considered easier times? I don't know. Today, that incinerator became my savior. My only choice. In a sea full of different outcomes and scenarios replaying in my mind, this had been my choice.

My glasses lay off to the side on the floor. I couldn't see without them, but from what I could see from here, they too were a shattered mess. Do you know how expensive eyeglasses are? Damn. I just bought them too, I saved my money from working at the Tunica Rivers Funeral Home. Mr. Dennis, the Funeral Director, and my boss, would know something had happened. He noticed everything and being that this was a funeral home, he could smell death a mile away. He said it lived in his blood, in his soul. How could death consume someone? He said his job was to *"see for the dead."* I wondered what he would see when he came in tomorrow morning. We would have to test his theory.

To no one important but me — it took one to three hours for a body to cremate. My mind replayed the sounds of Jaxon screaming as I turned the dial higher and higher until it reached 1800 Fahrenheit. My hands were shaking as I switched the large knob to the offsetting while the incinerator croaked to an end. *Like Jaxon,* I lamented. The old machine croaked to an end like Jaxon. I typically did my homework while I waited for the machine to do its thing, but this time, I couldn't account for those hours and I wasn't sure what had happened. Mr. Dennis was considering upgrading the machinery, but he never got around to it. His son Tyson also didn't keep the cleanest funeral home as I glanced around. This might help me ...

My phone buzzed somewhere in the room. It was slightly dark, and I heard it humming away, but I couldn't see it. Even though there was no one to call right now, anyway. I mean, what would I say? Hi there, I just killed Jaxon Green. The whitest white boy — and me — the blackest black girl. Yep, that would go over great. I knelt and searched around the corners until I found it lit up in the room's corner. My hands were shaking as I unlocked it. 10:46am. Jaxon had arrived at eight thirty.

Two hours.

That's about how long it took to annihilate Jaxon's body to nothing from the moment he walked in the door until it happened. And because Mr. Dennis' place was so dirty, Jaxon's body would hopefully be more debris added to the pile. A text message popped up from Malachi, my boyfriend.

Malachi: *Still comin' thru?*

I paused and stared at the wall. I planned to meet up with Malachi and our friends, Will and Mila. The four of us have been friends since elementary school. Will and Mila lived a few blocks from my house, and Malachi lived in West Tunica, on the outskirts of the city. They section the city off by zones and technically — the four of us should have never gone to the same school, but just our luck they modge podged us together. Malachi and I have been dating for one year. You would think we'd tire of each other, going to school together since Kindergarten and all, but it just made us closer. Today we were supposed to celebrate graduating from high school the day before. Today was supposed to be about making the most of our last summer before some of us went away to college. No, today was not supposed to begin with a murder.

A deep sigh escaped me, and I placed my phone back into my pocket, not responding to Malachi. Time was ticking, and now people were looking for me. Decisions needed to be made. I gazed around the room and saw nothing that would show Jaxon had been here. There wasn't much to clean up around the room; there wasn't much to do once a body burned, but I peered around anyway. I assessed the scene of the crime, my crime. Pulling the heavy door closed behind me, I turned out the lights and walked upstairs.

Jaxon's bag sat in Mr. Dennis's office. I froze and stared at it, trying to remember when he sat it there. Should I burn that too? Maybe. But I didn't want to go back down there right now. We needed some space from each other. I searched through his bag and I didn't find a cell phone. He must've had it with him in the incinerator. That meant it burned up too ... Good, one less thing to worry about. Rummaging through everything, I found a black and white notebook with my initials on the front, ITL-Indigo Tina Lewis. I flipped through the pages and heat washed over me. Jaxon wrote dozens of different things he was going to blackmail me with. Not only did he reference the pictures, (which partially brought him to his demise), but he had copies of my Dad's paystubs, my sister Sidney's last report card- and even my college acceptance letter. *What would he need with all that?* I fumed. He was plotting against me while I was trying to keep the peace. I closed the book and slid it into my bag for safekeeping.

What led us to this point? How did this happen? How did I end up killing Jaxon, when we just graduated from high school the day before? I thought about my dad and Sidney. They needed me, and I still had so much to do for them. Jaxon had brought this on himself and that book proved that. My hands were shaking as I collected Jaxon's bag and anything else that looked out of place. Standing in the center of the room, I tried to remember how it looked before Jaxon Green stepped foot through the door. Maybe it was my fault, I should've never told him to meet me at work. He pushed and pushed and pushed. At first it started with doing his homework, and that was okay. A fair exchange, I believed it to be at the time. Then he changed and wanted different things. Things I wasn't comfortable with. He talked to me like I was some jump off — and that I was not. I had enough of his shit and I saw red. Maybe there had been another option? I'm not sure. But it didn't present itself, and I did what I had to do. It was Friday, ten in the morning, and I was cleaning up a murder. Who was this person I was turning into?

Have you ever drove past a car accident? It stops traffic for miles and miles. Cars are backed up and honking at each other and then, when you finally creep your way to the scene, you realize it's not even that bad most of the time. So many people are driving and stopped to glimpse someone else's mistakes, creating a traffic jam. It was one of those things that couldn't be avoided. You couldn't help but watch a car accident. *Did anybody die? Was it anyone I know?* Maybe I was the only one who had thoughts like that, I guess. Jaxon was my car accident, and this accident was that bad. Mr. Dennis asked me to lock up when I was finished for the day and trusted me with the keys. I cremated dozens of bodies to prepare for services, but never anyone I knew. And never by my own hands.

I killed Jaxon. I killed nothing in my life, not even a bug. But Jaxon, Jaxon was important. Somewhere deep in my body, I felt nervous. But not the bad nervous that makes you question yourself and everything around

you — the good nervous when something happens and you're kinda sorta pleased. I would never say it out loud. I would dare not speak it, but listening to Jaxon's cries and watching his hand bang against the small incinerator window added extra pep to my step. My heart jumped with amazement.

Girls are expected to be dainty. Feminine; sugar and all spice. Fuck that shit. Respect me or be destroyed.

Made in the USA
Monee, IL
05 January 2022